Tales by the World's Great Contemporary Writers Presented Unabridged

All selections in
Short Story International
are reprinted full and
unabridged in the author's
own words. Nothing is
added, subtracted,
condensed or rewritten.

Editor
Sylvia Tankel

Associate Editor
Erik Sandberg-Diment

Contributing Editor
John Harr

Assitant Editors
Mildred Butterworth
Arlene Loveless
Kirsten Hammerle

Art Director
Mort Rubenstein

Drawings by
John Groth

Circulation Director
Nat Raboy

Production Director
Ludwig K. Marz

Business Manager
John O'Connor

Publisher
Sam Tankel

Volume 4, Number 21, August 1980.
Short Story International (USPS 375-970)
Copyright © by International Cultural
Exchange 1980. Printed in the U.S.A. All
rights reserved. Reproduction in whole or
in part prohibited. Second-class postage
paid at Great Neck, N.Y. 11022 and at
additional mailing offices. **Editorial
offices: P.O. Box 405, Great Neck,
N.Y. 11022.** Enclose stamped, self-
addressed envelope with previously
published stories submitted for possible
reprinting in *Short Story International*.
Please note *SSI* does not accept
unpublished original manuscripts. One
year (six issues) subscription for U.S.,
U.S. possessions $12, Canada $15, other
countries $17. Single copy price $2.95.
**For subscriptions and address
changes write to *Short Story
International*. P.O. Box 13913,
Philadelphia, Pa. 19104.** *Short Story
International* is published bimonthly by
International Cultural Exchange, 6
Sheffield Road, Great Neck, N.Y. 11021.
Postmaster please send Form 3579 to
P.O. Box 13913, Philadelphia, Pa.
19104.

Note from the Editor

Nobel laureate Isaac Bashevis Singer says, "I consider the short story the mainstay of literature. In no other field have the masters of literature achieved a greater perfection . . ." And no other country contributed more to the golden age of the short story than the USA, where such pioneers as Poe and Hawthorne and Washington Irving helped perfect the form, and O. Henry added his crowning touch.

It is good therefore to be able to report that in the United States the short story is receiving renewed attention—and not only because of contemporary masters like Mr. Singer himself, and others, including Joyce Carol Oates, John Cheever and John Updike. That most pervasive medium, television, has become an instrument of the resurgence of short stories. Public television's series, *The American Short Story,* has given millions of people the opportunity to witness dramatizations of short stories created by American grand masters.

This has been deservedly hailed, but it has an unnecessary limitation. The writers have not only been all American, they have been primarily from the past. If *The American Short Story* found interest in Nathaniel Hawthorne's tale of old Italy, *Rappacini's Daughter,* surely there are modern works from all points of the compass equally worthy of television attention.

One of the most rewarding aspects of *Short Story International* is that its contemporary stories transcend national limitations and touch the wellsprings of universal human understanding. Since short stories lend themselves admirably to adaptation, could not television series also enjoy that same wonderful privilege, by expanding its short story horizons to draw more from contemporary as well as deceased authors, and from all the world rather than our own small corner?

Copyrights and acknowledgments

We wish to express deep thanks to the authors, publishers, translators and literary agents for their permission to reprint the stories in this issue.

"A Boat-shaped Mind, A Man-shaped Soul . . ." from *The Electric Beach* by James McQueen. Copyright © 1978 James McQueen. Reprinted by permission of the author and Robin Books. "The Imitation of the Rose" (A Imitacao da Rose) from *Lacos de Familia* by Clarice Lispector. © 1960 Clarice Lispector. Translation by Giovanni Pontiero. English translation first appeared in *Family Ties* published by University of Texas Press. "The Turning Point" by Sheila Hodgson first appeared in *Blackwood's Magazine.* Reprinted by permission of the author and editor of *Blackwood's Magazine.* "The Conference" from *Alamaisen kyyneleet* by Erno Paasilinna. Translation by David Barrett in *Books from Finland.* Reprinted by permission of the author, Otava Publishing Company and the Information Centre for Finnish Literature. "Thank You, Dr. Coué" from *Most of All They Taught Me Happiness* by Rober Muller. Copyright © 1979 Robert G. Muller. Published by Doubleday & Company, Inc. "Tears for a Tailor" by E.G. Chipulina first appeared in *She.* Reprinted by permission of the author and the National Magazine Company Ltd. "Don Chepe" by Victor Perera first appeared in *Antioch Review.* Copyright 1979 Victor Perera. Reprinted by permission of the author. "The Elephant Stop" by G.S. Sharat Chandra first appeared in *Overland.* Copyright G.S. Sharat Chandra. "The Stranger" by Michael Foley from *Paddy No More.* Published by Longship Press. Copyright 1977 Michael Foley. "Marry a Greek" by Joy Cowley. Copyright 1977 Joy Cowley. "Rains" by Pira Sudham first appeared in *Bangkok Post.* Copyright 1979 Pira Sudham. "Lions, Kings and Dragons" by Margaret Perry first appeared in *Panache.* Copyright Margaret Perry. Reprinted by permission of the author, *Panache Magazine* & Panache, Inc. "The Ritual Bath" from *The Blue Door and Other Stories* by Lawrence P. Spingarn. Copyright © 1977 Lawrence P. Spingarn. "Moments" by Yuri Bondarev first appeared in *Soviet Literature,* 1977. Translation by Tamara Mats. Reprinted by permission of VAAP.

Photo credits: Erno Paasilinna © Jorma Komulainen. Michael Foley by Roy Alexander. Yuri Bondarev by Nicholas Kochnev © VAAP.

Table of Contents

"Hell . . . she must have been really something.
Look at that line . . ."

A Boat-shaped Mind, A Man-shaped Soul . . .

BY JAMES McQUEEN

The enchantment of a forlorn hulk of a boat.

WE never knew her name, or her age, or even where she came from. And we knew her only for a short time. But I've never forgotten her, and I'm sure the others haven't, either.

There were three of us, all under twenty; Harry was a clerk at the Railways, Peter worked for an insurance company, and I was a counterjumper in a menswear store. We'd grown up together—near the water—gone to school together, and when we'd left school and started work we'd gone on knocking about together. Mostly on or around the harbor, the river, the bay. In the end we'd raked up fifty quid each and bought a boat. That was the one big, important thing in our lives, the boat. She was no great beauty, a twenty-eight foot converted Montague whaler, clinker built, double-ended, with a suit of patched sails and an old Kelvin engine. No great beauty, as I say, not much headroom below decks, and no speed; but a fine, dry boat, built for work and rough water, and we scraped and painted and caulked until she was as neat and trim as anything at the yacht club's moorings.

We had a lot of fun in her, fishing, cruising, or just poking about the harbor. And sometimes we'd sail out into the open sea and cruise along the coast for a weekend. After a while it seemed to merge, all of it, into one single experience; now I find it difficult to separate one day from another. Except that some occasions seemed special; at least they seem special now, in retrospect. A night, for instance, at Whale Bay; a black night, absolutely pitch black, water and sky alike, the only relief in the blackness a tiny yellow glow from a cottage high on the hill; the cod beginning to bite just before midnight, running like mad for an hour while we filled empty kerosene tins with the fish; then going off the bite again, suddenly, just stopping like that; then the three of us sitting round the hatch drinking rum, letting the darkness and the cold close round us, smelling the hard salty sea smell, and the fresh fish smell, and the heavy fragrance of the black rum.

And the next morning, beating back up the estuary to the harbor, hugging the bank away from the chop of the tidal rip; morning light flat and yellow and cold, bouncing like golden snowflakes off the steel-blue water; Harry at the tiller, Peter swabbing down the deck to clear the fish slime; and me, bending over a primus at the open hatchway frying fish—the smallest of the cod—in a great pan of butter. Not a good table fish, the humble cod—yet I can't remember ever eating better fish than those crumbling, butter-glazed cod on that bright, bitter morning. Days like that hang fixed, somehow, in the memory.

But to get back to the other business . . . well, Harry saw her first, and Peter and I didn't hear about her until the next day, a Sunday. Harry turned up on his motor bike while Peter and I were painting the little dinghy that we carried on top of the deckhouse. We had it on the jetty between us, green paint slick and irridiscent in the sunlight, when he roared up and skidded to a stop below us. He'd been down the coast the day before to see some relatives, and hadn't been out on the boat with us. He propped the bike and clambered up.

"Listen," he said, "I think we can make a quid . . ."

We put down the paint brushes. At that stage I was earning seven quid a week, and there was never much left over after the rent was paid.

Harry began to roll a smoke, squatting on the gray boards. He was thin, intense, red-headed; really the leader, I suppose, if we had one. Not that it was ever discussed, it was just that, well, we tended to follow in the direction he went, most of the time.

"I was down Reigate way, seeing the brother-in-law, and I came back up the old coast road." He paused, squinting against the smoke. "Went into Spoon Bay, hadn't been there for years. Just to have a look. Listen, there's a boat there, propped up, just above high-water mark, beside an old shed. It was getting dark by the time I got there, but I had a quick look. She's a wreck, broken back, I think, but she's got a lot of lead on her keel . . . maybe a hundred quid's worth." His eyes were very blue and bright. "I found out who owns her—an old farmer—and I reckon we could buy her cheap, tow her away and strip her. What do you reckon?"

Peter was cautious. "If she's a wreck, how could we tow her away? It's nearly twenty miles."

Harry shook his head impatiently. "The planking's sound enough . . . we might have to caulk and bail a bit, but if we pick a calm day . . ."

We were silent for a few moments.

I asked the inevitable question. "How much?"

"Ten quid. I reckon if we offer ten quid . . ."

In the end we agreed to find the money, sail down and have a look. If she was sound enough, then we would try it. After all, it would only take a day to tow her in, and the weather was fairly settled.

We sailed down the next Saturday to look at her. From the sea we couldn't see much, the water in the bay was shallow, and we had to anchor a quarter of a mile offshore and scull in over the mudflats. But when we reached the beach we realized that Harry had been right. There was something wrong with the shape of the hull below the water line, a sort of warping, but she looked solid enough, and the planking seemed sound. She looked a wreck, though. We clambered aboard and stood unsteadily among the

11

weathered and splintered wreckage of the decking. She was about fifty feet long, and at least half a century old; a sloop, with an improbably heavy mast splintered and snapped off thirty feet above deck level. Most of the decking and fittings had been torn out long ago, and she was really little more than a shell. But the shell seemed firm enough, and a little rough caulking would make her fairly watertight.

"Well?" asked Harry.

Peter and I looked at each other quickly. Peter climbed over the side and had another look at the keel. Then he looked at me again, very dark and serious. And nodded slowly.

So we went to see the farmer.

In the end he settled for eight pounds; Harry was a keen bargainer.

The next weekend we went down to collect her. We spent the Saturday afternoon caulking and patching, and working out how we were going to get her into the water. We slept on our own boat that night, and started the next morning. Actually, it was easier than we had expected. The touchy part was clearing her from the props without damaging the hull. But we managed that, and then rigged a block and tackle to a heavy pile fifty feet below the tide mark and winched her slowly into the water.

That was when we first noticed her, really, as she settled herself and steadied in the water. We gathered, wet and muddy, at the water's edge and looked at her.

"Hell," said Peter, "she must have been really something. Look at that line . . ."

He was right, she must have been something. I could imagine her, with fresh paint and white sails and polished brightwork . . .

Harry wiped mud from his face. "Yeah, well, she's worth the lead on her keel now. That's all."

We climbed into the dinghy and started to fix the tow line.

When we got under way Peter and I stayed in her to bail while Harry sailed our boat. The weather was good, the sea smooth, and we made fair time up the coast and into the channel. All the same it was dark by the time we reached our mooring. There'd been no trouble; we'd had to bail steadily for the first hour or so, but then the dry timbers had started to take up water and the planking had swelled and closed the seams. After that she was pretty near watertight, what with our caulking and all.

But it was late, and cold, and we decided that we'd have to wait until the next weekend to beach her and start the job of stripping. So we left her at the mooring, bobbing gently in the darkness, and puttered off upstream to anchor near the oil wharf.

I didn't see her again until the middle of the week, but Harry came in on Monday night to tell me that he'd been down to check her, and she was making almost no water and was safe and dry.

"We'll start Saturday morning, alright?"

But I wanted to see her again before then. I don't quite know why. Or I didn't then. So on the Wednesday after work I walked down to the river. By the time I got there the fog had come down fairly thickly, and I couldn't see more than a hundred yards. When I got to the jetty I thought for one panicky moment that she was gone. But then I saw her, indistinct in the fog, riding easily at the mooring.

It was a shock. Because in the half darkness and the mist it seemed that fifty years of wear and tear and abuse had fallen away from her. The missing mast top was barely noticeable, and the torn timbers and scabby hull were disguised and covered by the night and fog. She lay beam on to the shore, moving lightly in the current; and standing there on the bare, cold jetty, hunched in my overcoat, I felt a painful excitement in my throat. Because she was suddenly very beautiful, and the sight of that heartbreakingly lovely line of her sheer brought strange pricklings to the backs of my eyes.

I watched her for a long time, filled with all sorts of half-understood emotions. There is something about a boat, any boat, that reaches out and touches the most land-bound of us. And this boat was something special. After a while I was conscious of someone standing beside me. I turned to see Harry, the collar of his windcheater pulled up around his ears.

"Can't we do something?" I asked. "Fix her up, somehow?"

He shook his head. "Her back's broken. She's finished." He wiped a bead from the end of his nose. "Peter asked me the same thing last night." He turned away. "See you Saturday morning."

But he didn't sound happy.

I was late that Saturday morning. Somehow I had been reluctant to crawl out of bed, to start the day. The thought of the money we would get was suddenly distasteful, and the work of beaching and wrecking would be . . . just work. But eventually I dragged myself out, made toast and tea, and caught a bus down to the river.

The mooring was empty. Just the buoy bobbing on the tide. I stood, puzzled, on the jetty, wondering if they had left without me, and if I had better catch a bus round to the beach where we had planned to take her. Then I heard footsteps behind me. It was Peter.

"Where is she?" I asked.

"Come up here." He jerked his head at the steps leading up to the top of the bank above the slips. I followed him up the rickety wooden stairs. We stood at the top, looking out over the bay. He pointed. Far away, maybe a couple of miles, I could see two boats, close together.

"It's Harry," said Peter. "He's got her in tow. He was just leaving when I got here. I shouted, but he didn't answer."

"But he's headed . . . nowhere. Out to sea."

He nodded. "Come on, we'll have a cuppa up the road."

We waited around all day in the cold. At lunchtime we bought a couple of pies and retired to the pub along the road. There was a big open fire in the bar, and we sat there until nearly five o'clock, making our drinks stretch, wandering out every half hour or so to see if there was any sign of Harry. In the late afternoon the wind began to get up, gusting in from the west. Our side of the river was sheltered, in the lee of the hill, but we could see the wind cutting the tops off the waves further out, short ugly scuts of white on the leaden water.

Finally, an hour before dark, we sighted the boat—just one boat—a couple of miles out, making slow work against the wind and chop. We could see it pitching and corkscrewing. We went down to the jetty to watch him come in. He ran neatly up to the buoy, picked up the mooring, and sculled in looking pinched and cold. He turned once to look back down the estuary, where night was closing in.

He flung the painter up, and I caught it.

"Where is she?" asked Peter. "What have you done with her?"

Harry said nothing, just clambered up and stood beside me, blue and shaking with cold.

We were silent. At last Harry spoke. "Come on," he said, pushing his hands deep in the pockets of his jacket, "I need rum."

We followed him up the steps and across the road.

Inside the pub we waited till he had downed the first rum and the shivering had diminished a little.

"Well," I said, "what *have* you done with her?"

He turned and looked at me fiercely, the blue eyes very hard and bright behind the cold-reddened lids.

"I towed her ten miles out to sea and turned her loose . . ."

He turned back to the bar, head down. He looked very tired.

"She won't last long in this," said Peter, cocking his head to listen. The wind was up to maybe thirty-five knots and getting stronger. I found myself sighing deeply, thinking of her out there in the open sea, thinking of the caulking going, the planks springing, the sea surging in, the hull sinking lower and lower in the water, the great waves rolling over her . . .

"Three rums," said Harry to the barman.

We stood there, saying nothing, drinking our rum, and although I felt a great sadness, I felt, too, as if a great weight had been suddenly lifted off me. I touched Harry on the shoulder to let him know that it was all right, and I noticed that for a while Peter stayed very close to him, as if to reassure him.

Five years ago, on turning 40, James McQueen relinquished a career as a mining company executive and started writing full time. He is a dedicated, prodigious writer, widely published in Australian literary journals and magazines, whose literary prizes include several State of Victoria Short Story Awards.

"But in her humble opinion, the one
command seemed to cancel out the other,
as if they were asking her to eat flour
and whistle at the same time."

The Imitation of the Rose

BY CLARICE LISPECTOR

A love of beauty and perfection . . . with psychological twists.

BEFORE Armando came home from work the house would have to be tidied and Laura herself ready in her brown dress so that she could attend her husband while he dressed, and then they would leave at their leisure, arm in arm as in former times. How long was it since they had last done that?

But now that she was "well" again, they would take the bus, she looking like a wife, watching out of the bus window, her arm in his: and later they would dine with Carlota and João, sitting back intimately in their chairs. How long was it since she had seen Armando sit back with intimacy and converse with another man? A man at peace was one who, oblivious of his wife's presence, could converse with another man about the latest news in the headlines. Meantime, she would talk to Carlota about women's things, submissive to the authoritarian and practical goodness of Carlota, receiving once more her friend's attention and vague

17

disdain, her natural abruptness, instead of that perplexed affection full of curiosity —watching Armando, finally oblivious of his own wife. And she herself, finally returning to play an insignificant role with gratitude. Like a cat which, having spent the night out of doors, as if nothing had happened, had unexpectedly found a saucer of milk waiting. People fortunately helped to make her feel that she was "well" again. Without watching her, they actively helped her to forget, they themselves feigning forgetfulness as if they had read the same directions on the same medicine bottle. Or, perhaps, they had really forgotten. How long was it since she last saw Armando sit back with abandon, oblivious of her presence? And she herself?

Interrupting her efforts to tidy up the dressing table, Laura gazed at herself in the mirror. And she herself? How long had it been? Her face had a domestic charm, her hair pinned behind her large pale ears. Her brown eyes and brown hair, her soft dark skin, all lent to that face, no longer so very young, the unassuming expression of a woman. Perhaps someone might have seen in that ever so tiny hint of surprise in the depths of her eyes, perhaps someone might have seen in that ever so tiny hint of sorrow the lack of children which she never had?

With her punctilious liking for organization—that same inclination which had made her as a school-girl copy out her class notes in perfect writing without ever understanding them—to tidy up the house before the maid had her afternoon off so that, once Maria went out, she would have nothing more to do except (1) calmly get dressed; (2) wait for Armando once she was ready; (3) what was the third thing? Ah yes. That was exactly what she would do. She would wear her brown dress with the cream lace collar. Having already had her bath. Even during her time at the Sacred Heart Convent she had always been tidy and clean, with an obsession for personal hygiene and a certain horror of disorder. A fact which never caused Carlota, who was already a little odd even as a school girl, to admire her. The reactions of the two women had always been different. Carlota ambitious and laughing heartily; Laura, a little slow, and virtually always taking care to be slow. Carlota, seeing danger in nothing; and Laura ever cautious. When they had given her *The Imitation of Christ* to read, with the zeal of a donkey she had read the book without understanding it, but may God forgive her, she had felt that anyone who imitated Christ would be lost —lost in the light, but dangerously lost. Christ was the worst temptation. And Carlota, who had not even attempted to read it, had lied to the Sister, saying that she had finished it.

That was decided. She would wear her brown dress with the cream collar made of real lace.

But when she saw the time, she remembered with alarm, causing her to raise her hand to her breast, that she had forgotten to drink her glass of milk.

She made straight for the kitchen and, as if she had guiltily betrayed Armando and their devoted friends through her neglect, standing by the refrigerator she took the first sips with anxious pauses, concentrating upon each sip with faith as if she were compensating everyone and showing her repentance.

When the doctor had said, "Take milk between your meals, and avoid an empty stomach because that causes anxiety," then, even without the threat of anxiety, she took her milk without further discussion, sip by sip, day by day—she never failed, obeying blindly with a touch of zeal, so that she might not perceive in herself the slightest disbelief. The embarrassing thing was that the doctor appeared to contradict himself, for while giving precise instructions that she chose to follow with the zeal of a convert, he had also said, "Relax! Take things easy; don't force yourself to succeed—completely forget what has happened and everything will return to normal." And he had given her a pat on the back that had pleased her and made her blush with pleasure.

But in her humble opinion, the one command seemed to cancel out the other, as if they were asking her to eat flour and whistle at the same time. In order to fuse both commands into one, she had invented a solution: that glass of milk which had finished up by gaining a secret power, which almost embodied with every sip the taste of a word and renewed that firm pat on the back, that glass of milk she carried into the sitting room where she sat "with great naturalness," feigning a lack of interest, "not forcing herself"— and thereby cleverly complying with the second order. It doesn't matter if I get fat, she thought, beauty has never been the most important thing.

She sat down on the couch as if she were a guest in her own home, which, so recently regained, tidy and impersonal, recalled the peace of a stranger's house. A feeling that gave her great satisfaction: the opposite of Carlota who had made of her home something similar to herself. Laura experienced such pleasure in making something impersonal of her home; in a certain way perfect, because impersonal.

Oh, how good it was to be back, to be truly back, she smiled with satisfaction. Holding the almost empty glass, she closed her eyes with a pleasureable weariness. She had ironed Armando's shirts, she had prepared methodical lists for the following day, she had calculated in detail what she had spent at the market that morning; she had not paused, in fact, for a single minute. Oh, how good it was to be tired again!

If some perfect creature were to descend from the planet Mars and discover that people on the Earth were tired and growing old, he would feel pity and dismay. Without ever understanding what was good about being people, about feeling tired and failing daily; only the initiated would understand this nuance of depravity and refinement of life.

And she had returned at last from the perfection of the planet Mars. She, who had never had any ambitions except to be a wife to some man, gratefully returned to find her share of what is daily fallible. With her eyes closed she sighed gratefully. How long was it since she had felt tired? But now every day she felt almost exhausted. She had ironed, for example, Armando's shirts; she had always enjoyed ironing and, modesty aside, she pressed clothes to perfection. And afterward she felt exhausted as a sort of compensation. No longer to feel that alert lack of fatigue. No longer to feel that point—empty, aroused, and nideously exhilarating within oneself. No longer to feel that terrible independence. No longer that monstrous and simple facility of not sleeping—neither by day nor by night—which in her discretion had suddenly made her superhuman by comparison with her tired and perplexed husband. Armando, with that offensive breath which he developed when he was silently preoccupied, stirring in her a poignant compassion, yes, even within her alert perfection, her feeling and love . . . she, superhuman and tranquil in her bright isolation, and he—when he had come to visit her timidly bringing apples and grapes that the nurse, with a shrug of her shoulders, used to eat—he visiting her ceremoniously like a lover with heavy breath and fixed smile, forcing himself in his heroism to try to understand . . . he who had received her from a father and a clergyman, and who did not know what to do with this girl from Tijuca, who unexpectedly, like a tranquil boat spreading its sails over the waters, had become superhuman.

But now it was over. All over. Oh, it had been a mere weakness: temperament was the worst temptation. But later she had recovered so completely that she had even started once more to exercise care not to plague others with her former obsession for detail. She could well remember her companions at the convent saying to her, "That's the thousandth time you've counted that!" She remembered them with an uneasy smile.

She had recovered completely: now she was tired every day, every day her face sagged as the afternoon wore on, and the night then assumed its old finality and became more than just a perfect starry night. And everything completed itself harmoniously. And, as for the whole world, each day fatigued her; as for the whole world, human and perishable. No longer that thing which one day had clearly spread like a cancer . . . her soul.

She opened her eyes heavy with sleep, feeling the consoling solidity of the glass in her hand, but closed them again with a comfortable smile of fatigue, bathing herself like a *nouveau riche* in all his wealth, in this familiar and slightly nauseating water. Yes, slightly nauseating: what did it matter? For if she, too, was a little nauseating, she was fully aware of it. But her husband didn't think so and then what did it matter, for happily she did not live in surroundings which demanded that she should be more clever and interesting, she was even free of school which so embarrassingly had demanded that she should be alert. What did it matter? In exhaustion —she had ironed Armando's shirts without mentioning that she had been to the market in the morning and

21

had spent some time there with that delight she took in making things yield—in exhaustion she found a refuge, that discreet and obscure place from where, with so much constraint toward herself and others, she had once departed. But as she was saying, fortunately she had returned.

And if she searched with greater faith and love she would find within her exhaustion that even better place, which would be sleep. She sighed with pleasure, for one moment of mischievous malice tempted to go against that warm breath she exhaled, already inducing sleep . . . for one moment tempted to doze off. "Just for a moment, only one tiny moment!" she pleaded with herself, pleased at being so tired, she pleaded persuasively, as one pleads with a man, a facet of her behavior that had always delighted Armando. But she did not really have time to sleep now, not even to take a nap, she thought smugly and with false modesty. She was such a busy person! She had always envied those who could say "I couldn't find the time," and now once more she was such a busy person.

They were going to dinner at Carlota's house, and everything had to be organized and ready, it was her first dinner out since her return and she did not wish to arrive late, she had to be ready. "Well, I've already said this a thousand times," she thought with embarrassment. It would be sufficient to say it only once. "I did not wish to arrive late." For this was a sufficient reason: if she had never been able to bear without enormous vexation giving trouble to anyone, now more than ever, she should not. No, no, there was not the slightest doubt: she had no time to sleep. What she must do, stirring herself with familiarity in that intimate wealth of routine—and it hurt her that Carlota should despise her liking for routine—what she must do was (1) wait until the maid was ready; (2) give her the money so that she could bring the meat in the morning, top round of beef; how could she explain that the difficulty of finding good meat was, for her, really an interesting topic of conversation, but if Carlota were to find out, she would despise her; (3) to begin washing and dressing herself carefully, surrendering, without reservations to the pleasure of making the most of the time at her disposal. Her brown dress matched her eyes, and her collar in cream lace gave her an almost childlike appearance, like some child from the past. And, back in the nocturnal peace of Tijuca, no longer that dazzling light of ebullient nurses, their hair carefully set, going out to enjoy themselves after having tossed her like a helpless chicken into the void of insulin—back to the nocturnal peace of Tijuca, restored to her real life.

She would go out arm in arm with Armando, walking slowly to the bus stop with those low thick hips which her girdle parceled into one, transforming her into a striking woman. But when she awkwardly explained to Armando that this resulted from ovarian insufficiency, Armando, who liked his wife's hips, would saucily retort, "What good would it do me to be married to a ballerina?" That was how he responded. No one would have suspected it, but at times Armando could be extremely devious. From time to time they repeated the same phrases. She explained that it was on account of ovarian insufficiency. Then he would retort, "What good would it do me to be married to a ballerina?" At times he was shameless and no one would have suspected it.

Carlota would have been horrified if she were to know that they, too, had an intimate life and shared things she could not discuss, but nevertheless she regretted not being able to discuss them. Carlota certainly thought that she was only neat and ordinary and a little boring; but if she were obliged to take care in order not to annoy the others with details, with Armando she let herself go at times and became boring. Not that this mattered because, although he pretended to listen, he did not absorb everything she told him. Nor did she take offense, because she understood perfectly well that her conversation rather bored other people, but it was nice to be able to tell him that she had been able to find good meat, even if Armando shook his head and did not listen. She and the maid conversed a great deal, in fact more so she than the maid, and she was careful not to bother the maid, who at times suppressed her impatience and became somewhat rude—the fault was really hers because she did not always command respect.

But, as she was saying . . . her arm in his, she short and he tall and thin, though he was healthy, thank God, and she was chestnut-haired. Chestnut-haired as she obscurely felt a wife ought to be. To have black or blonde hair was an exaggeration, which, in her desire to make the right choice, she had never wanted. Then, as for green eyes, it seemed to her that if she had green eyes it would be as if she had not told her husband everything. Not that Carlota had given cause for any scandal, although Laura, were she given the opportunity, would hotly defend her, but the opportunity had never arisen. She, Laura, was obliged reluctantly to agree that her friend had a strange and amusing manner of treating her husband, not because "they treated each other as equals," since this was now common enough, but you know what I mean to say. And Carlota was even a little different, even she had remarked on this once to Armando and Armando had agreed without attaching much importance to the fact. But, as she was saying, in brown with the lace collar . . . her reverie filled her with the same pleasure she experienced when tidying out drawers, and she even found herself disarranging them in order to tidy them up again.

She opened her eyes and, as if it were the room that had taken a nap and not she, the room seemed refurbished and refreshed with its chairs brushed and its curtains, which had shrunk in the last washing, looking like trousers that are too short and the wearer looking comically at his own legs. Oh! how good it was to see everything tidy again and free of dust, everything cleaned by her own capable hands, and so silent and with a vase of flowers as in a waiting room. She had always found waiting rooms pleasing, so respectful and impersonal. How satisfying life together was, for her who had at last returned from extravagance. Even a vase of flowers. She looked at it.

"Ah! how lovely they are," her heart exclaimed suddenly, a bit childish. They were small wild roses which she had bought that morning at the market, partly because the man had insisted so much, partly out of daring. She had arranged them in a vase that very morning, while drinking her sacred glass of milk at ten o'clock.

But in the light of this room the roses stood in all their complete and tranquil beauty. "Have I ever seen such lovely roses?" she thought enquiringly. And, as if she had not just been thinking precisely this, vaguely aware that she had been thinking precisely this, and quickly dismissing her embarrassment upon recognizing herself as being a little tedious, she thought in a newer phase of surprise, "Really, I have never seen such pretty roses." She looked at them attentively. But her attention could not be sustained for very long as simple attention, and soon transformed itself into soothing pleasure, and she was no longer able to analyze the roses and felt obliged to interrupt herself with the same exclamation of submissive enquiry: "How lovely they are!"

They were a bouquet of perfect roses, several on the same stem. At some moment they had climbed with quick eagerness over each other but then, their game over, they had become tranquilly immobilized. They were quite perfect roses in their minuteness, not quite open, and their pink hue was almost white. "They seem almost artificial," she uttered in surprise. They might give the impression of being white if they were completely open, but with the center petals curled in a bud, their color was concentrated and, as in the lobe of an ear, one could sense the redness circulate inside them. "How lovely they are," thought Laura, surprised. But without knowing why, she felt somewhat restrained and a little perplexed. Oh, nothing serious, it was only that such extreme beauty disturbed her.

She heard the maid's footsteps on the brick floor of the kitchen, and from the hollow sound she realized that she was wearing high heels and that she must be ready to leave. Then Laura had an idea which was in some way highly original: why not ask Maria to call at Carlota's house and leave the roses as a present?

And also because that extreme beauty disturbed her. Disturbed her? It was a risk. Oh! no, why a risk? It merely disturbed her; they were a warning. Oh! no, why a warning? Maria would deliver the roses to Carlota.

"Dona Laura sent them," Maria would say. She smiled thoughtfully: Carlota would be puzzled that Laura, being able to bring the roses personally, since she wanted to present them to her, should send them before dinner with the maid. Not to mention that she would find it amusing to receive the roses . . . and would think it "refined."

"These things aren't necessary between us, Laura!" the other would say with that frankness of hers which was somewhat tactless, and Laura would exclaim in a subdued cry of rapture, "Oh, no! no! It is not because of the invitation to dinner! It is because the roses are so lovely that I felt the impulse to give them to you!"

Yes, if at the time the opportunity arose and she had the courage, that was exactly what she would say. What exactly would she say? It was important not to forget. She would say, "Oh, no! no! It is not because of the invitation to dinner! It is because the roses are so lovely that I felt the impulse to give them to you!"

And Carlota would be surprised at the delicacy of Laura's sentiments—no one would imagine that Laura, too, had her ideas. In this imaginary and pleasurable scene which made her smile devoutly, she addressed herself as "Laura," as if speaking to a third person. A third person full of that gentle, rustling, pleasant, and tranquil faith, Laura, the one with the real lace collar, dressed discreetly, the wife of Armando, an Armando, after all, who no longer needed to force himself to pay attention to all of her conversation about the maid and the meat . . . who no longer needed to think about his wife, like a man who is happy, like a man who is not married to a ballerina.

"I couldn't help sending you the roses," Laura would say, this third person so, but so . . . And to give the roses was almost as nice as the roses themselves.

And she would even be rid of them.

And what exactly would happen next? Ah yes; as she was saying, Carlota, surprised at Laura who was neither intelligent nor good but who had her secret feelings. And Armando? Armando would look at her with a look of real surprise —for it was essential to remember that he must not know the maid had taken the roses in the afternoon! Armando would look with kindness upon the impulses of his little wife and that night they would sleep together.

And she would have forgotten the roses and their beauty. No, she suddenly thought, vaguely warned. It was necessary to take care with that alarmed look in others. It was necessary never to cause them alarm, especially with everything being so fresh in their minds. And, above all, to spare everyone the least anxiety or doubt. And that the attention of others should no longer be necessary—no longer this horrible feeling of their watching her in silence, and her in their presence. No more impulses.

But at the same time she saw the empty glass in her hand and she also thought, " 'He' said that I should not force myself to succeed, that I should not think of adopting attitudes merely to show that I am."

"Maria," she called, upon hearing the maid's footsteps once more. And when Maria appeared she asked with a note of rashness and defiance, "Would you call at Dona Carlota's house and leave these roses for her? Just say that Dona Laura sent them. Just say it like that. Dona Laura . . ."

" 'Yes, I know," the maid interrupted her patiently.

Laura went to search for an old sheet of tissue paper. Then she carefully lifted the roses from the vase, so lovely and tranquil, with their delicate and mortal thorns. She wanted to make a really artistic bouquet: and at the same time she would be rid of them. And she would be able to dress and resume her day. When she had arranged the moist blooms in a bouquet, she held the flowers away from her and examined them at a distance, slanting her head and half-closing her eyes for an impartial and severe judgment.

And when she looked at them, she saw the roses. And then, irresistibly gentle, she insinuated to herself, "Don't give the roses away, they are so lovely."

A second later, still very gentle, her thought suddenly became slightly more intense, almost tempting, "Don't give them away, they are yours." Laura became a little frightened: because things were never hers.

But these roses were. Rosy, small, and perfect: they were hers. She looked at them, incredulous: they were beautiful and they were hers. If she could think further ahead, she would think: hers as nothing before now had ever been.

And she could even keep them because that initial uneasiness had passed which had caused her vaguely to avoid looking at the roses too much.

"Why give them away then? They are so lovely and you are

giving them away? So when you find something nice, you just go and give it away? Well, if they were hers," she insinuated persuasively to herself, without finding any other argument beyond the previous one which, when repeated, seemed to her to be ever more convincing and straightforward.

"They would not last long—why give them away then, so long as they were alive?" The pleasure of possessing them did not represent any great risk, she pretended to herself, because, whether she liked it or not, shortly she would be forced to deprive herself of them and then she would no longer think about them, because by then they would have withered.

"They would not last long; why give them away then?" The fact that they would not last long seemed to free her from the guilt of keeping them, in the obscure logic of the woman who sins. Well, one coud see that they would not last long (it would be sudden, without danger). And it was not even, she argued in a final and victorious rejection of guilt, she herself who had wanted to buy them; the flower seller had insisted so much and she always became so intimidated when they argued with her . . . It was not she who had wanted to buy them . . . she was not to blame in the slightest. She looked at them in rapture, thoughtful and profound.

"And, honestly, I never saw such perfection in all my life."

All right, but she had already spoken to Maria and there would be no way of turning back. Was it too late then? She became frightened upon seeing the tiny roses that waited impassively in her own hand. If she wanted, it would not be too late . . . She could say to Maria, "Oh, Maria, I have decided to take the roses myself when I go to dinner this evening!" And of course she would not take them . . . And Maria need never know. And, before changing, she would sit on the couch for a moment, just for a moment, to contemplate them. To contemplate that tranquil impassivity of the roses. Yes, because having already done the deed, it would be better to profit from it . . . she would not be foolish enough to take the blame without the profit. That was exactly what she would do.

But with the roses unwrapped in her hand she waited. She did not arrange them in the vase, nor did she call Maria. She knew why. Because she must give them away. Oh, she knew why.

And also because something nice was either for giving or receiving, not only for possessing. And above all, never for one *to be*. Above all, one should never *be* a lovely thing. A lovely thing lacked the gesture of giving. One should never keep a lovely thing, as if it were guarded within the perfect silence of one's heart. (Although, if she were not to give the roses, would anyone ever find out? It was horribly easy and within one's reach to keep them, for who would find out? And they would be hers, and things would stay as they were and the matter would be forgotten . . .)

"Well then? Well then?" she mused, vaguely disturbed.

Well, no. What she must do was to wrap them up and send them, without any pleasure now; to parcel them up and, disappointed, send them; and, terrified, be rid of them. Also, because a person had to be coherent, one's thoughts had to be consistent: if, spontaneously, she had decided to relinquish them to Carlota, she should stand by the decision and give them away. For no one changed their mind from one minute to another.

But anyone can repent, she suddenly rebelled. For if it was only the minute I took hold of the rises that I noticed how lovely they were, for the first time, actually, as I held them, I noticed how lovely they were. Or a little before that? (And they were really hers.) And even the doctor himself had patted her on the back and said, "Don't force yourself into pretending that you are well, because you *are* well!" And then that hearty pat on the back. So she was not obliged, therefore, to be consistent, she didn't have to prove anything to anyone, and she would keep the roses. (And in all sincerity —in all sincerity they were hers.)

"Are they ready?" Maria asked.

"Yes," said Laura, surprised.

She looked at them so mute in her hand. Impersonal in their extreme beauty. In their extreme and perfect tranquility as roses. That final instance: the flower. That final perfection; its luminous tranquility.

Like someone depraved, she watched with vague longing the tempting perfection of the roses . . . with her mouth a little dry, she watched them.

Until, slowly, austerely, she wrapped the stems and thorns in the tissue paper. She was so absorbed that only upon holding out the bouquet she had prepared did she notice that Maria was no longer in the room—and she remained alone with her heroic sacrifice.

Vacantly, sorrowfully, she watched them, distant as they were at the end of her outstretched arm—and her mouth became even dryer, parched by that envy and desire.

"But they are mine," she said with enormous timidity.

When Maria returned and took hold of the bouquet, for one tiny moment of greed Laura drew back her hand, keeping the roses to herself for one more second—they are so lovely and they are mine—the first lovely thing and mine! And it was the flower seller who had insisted . . . I did not go looking for them! It was destiny that had decreed! Oh, only this once! Only this once and I swear never more! (She could at least take one rose for herself, no more than this! One rose for herself. And only she would know and then never more; oh, she promised herself that never more would she allow herself to be tempted by perfection, never more.)

And the next moment, without any transition, without any obstacle, the roses were in the maid's hand, they were no longer hers, like a letter already in the post! One can no longer recover or obliterate statements! There is no point in shouting, "That was not what I wanted to say!" Her hands were now empty but her heart, obstinate and resentful, was still saying, "You can catch Maria on the stairs, you know perfectly well that you can, and take the roses from her hand and steal them—because to take them now would be to steal them." To steal what was hers? For this was what a person without any feeling for others would do: he would steal what was his by right! Have pity, dear God. You can get them back, she insisted, enraged. And then the front door slammed.

Slowly, she sat down calmly on the couch. Without leaning back. Only to rest. No, she was no longer angry, not even a little. But that tiny wounded spot in the depths of her eyes was larger and thoughtful. She looked at the vase.

"Where are my roses?" she said then very quietly.

And she missed the roses. They had left an empty space inside her. Remove an object from a clean table and by the cleaner patch which remains one sees that there has been dust all around it. The roses had left a patch without dust and without sleep inside her. In her heart, that one rose, which at least she could have taken for herself without prejudicing anyone in the world, was gone. Like something missing. Indeed, like some great loss. An absence that flooded into her like a light. And also around the mark left by the roses the dust was disappearing. The center of fatigue opened itself into a circle that grew larger. As if she had not ironed a single shirt for Armando. And in the clearing they had left, one missed those roses.

"Where are my roses?" she moaned without pain, smoothing the pleats of her skirt.

Like lemon juice dripping into dark tea and the dark tea becoming completely clear, her exhaustion gradually became clearer. Without, however, any tiredness. Just as the firefly alights. Since she was no longer tired, she was on the point of getting up to dress. It was time to start getting ready.

With parched lips, she tried for an instant to imitate the roses deep down inside herself. It was not even difficult.

It was just as well that she did not feel tired. In this way she would go out to dinner feeling more refreshed. Why not wear her cameo brooch on her cream-colored collar? The one the Major had brought back from the war in Italy. It would add a final touch to her neckline. When she was ready she would hear the noise of Armando's key in the door. She must get dressed. But it was still early. With the rush-hour traffic, he would be late in arriving. It was still afternoon. An extremely beautiful afternoon. But, in fact, it was no longer afternoon. It was evening. From the street there arose the first sounds of darkness and the first lights.

Moreover, the key penetrated with familiarity the keyhole.

Armando would open the door. He would press the light switch. And suddenly in the frame of the doorway that face would appear, betraying an expectancy he tried to conceal but could not restrain. Then his breathless suspense would finally transform itself into a smile of utter relief. That embarrassed smile of relief which he would never suspect her of noticing. That relief which, probably with a pat on the back, they had advised her poor husband to conceal. But which had been, for this woman whose heart was filled with guilt, her daily recompense for having restored to her husband the possibility of happiness and peace, sanctified at the hands of an austere priest who only permitted submissive happiness to humans and not the imitation of Christ.

The key turned in the lock, that dark, expectant face entered, and a powerful light flooded the room.

And in the doorway, Armando himself stopped short with that breathless expression as if he had run for miles in order to arrive in time. She was about to smile. So that she might dispel the anxious expectancy on his face, which always came mixed with the childish victory of having arrived in time to find his boring, good-hearted, and diligent wife. She was about to smile so that once more he might know that there would no longer be any danger in his arriving too late. She was about to smile in order to teach him gently to confide in her. It had been useless to advise them never to touch on the subject: they did not speak about it but they had created a language of facial expressions whereby fear and confidence were communicated, and question and answer were silently telegraphed. She was about to smile. She was taking her time, but meant to smile.

Calmly and sweetly she said, "It came back, Armando. It came back."

As if he would never understand, he averted his smiling, distrusting face. His main task for the moment was to try and control his breathless gasps after running up the stairs, now that, triumphantly, he had arrived in time, now that she was there to smile at him. As if he would never understand.

"What came back?" he finally asked her in an expressionless tone.

But while he was seeking never to understand, the man's face, ever more full of suspense, had already understood without a single feature having altered. His main task was to gain time and to concentrate upon controlling his breath. Which suddenly was no longer difficult. For unexpectedly he noticed to his horror that the room and the woman were calm and showing no signs of haste.

Still more suspicious, like someone about to end up howling with laughter upon observing something absurd, he meantime insisted upon keeping his face averted, from where he spied her cautiously, almost her enemy. And from where he already began to feel unable to restrain himself, from seeing her seated with her hands folded on her lap, with the serenity of the firefly that is alight.

In her innocent, chestnut gaze, the embarrassed vanity of not having been able to resist.

"What came back?" he asked suddenly with severity.

"I couldn't help myself," she said and her final compassion for this man was in her voice, one last appeal for pardon which already came mingled with the arrogance of an almost perfect solitude.

"I couldn't prevent it," she repeated, surrendering to him with relief the compassion which she with some effort had been able to contain until he arrived.

"It was on account of the roses," she said modestly.

As if a photograph were about to capture that moment, he still maintained the same disinterested expression, as if the photographer had asked him only for his face and not his soul. He opened his mouth and involuntarily his face took on for an instant an expression of comic detachment which he had used to conceal his annoyance when he had asked his boss for an increase in salary. The next moment, he averted his eyes, mortified by his wife's shamelessness as she sat there unburdened and serene.

But suddenly the tension fell. His shoulders dropped, the features of his face relaxed and a great heaviness settled over him. Aged and strange, he watched her.

She was seated wearing her little housedress. He knew that she had done everything possible not to become luminous and remote. With fear and respect he watched her. Aged, tired, and strange. But he did not even have a word to offer. From the open door he saw his wife sitting upright on the couch, once more alert and tranquil as if on a train. A train that had already departed.

Born 1925 in the Ukraine, Clarice Lispector's family emigrated to Brazil when she was two months old. Her interest in literature started early, she began writing short stories and plays while in her teens. In 1944 she graduated from the National Faculty of Law, was married and had her first novel, Perto do Coração Selvagem, published. Admiring critics generally agree her true medium is the short story. Clarice Lispector's work is strongly influenced by Sartre's existentialism. "The Imitation of the Rose" was sensitively translated by Giovanni Pontiero of the University of Manchester.

"Night found them crouched
amongst the ruins with their treasure,
still undecided as to the meaning
of the thing."

The Turning Point

BY SHEILA HODGSON

**Given the name without the gain,
two innocents dabble in witchcraft.**

I have written many ghost stories—I never cared to try any other
kind—and the question arises, do I believe in ghosts? Well, I am
prepared to consider evidence and accept it if I am satisfied. The
same criterion may fairly be applied to witchcraft, though here we
move on to somewhat sounder ground, there being more docu-
mentation and a larger volume of recorded fact; I am thinking in
particular of the strange history concerning Master Nicholas Palgrave. I first came across this in a collection of letters written in the
spring of 1549 by Sir John Cheke to his friend Sir William Butts of
Thornage, Norfolk. The correspondence actually relates to two
Cambridge students, Nicholas Palgrave and Chauncey Adam,
who had the grave misfortune in those turbulent years to be accused of conspiring with a notorious witch—but let me transcribe a
portion of Sir John's epistle.

"Having been made Aquaint of Lamentable Trafficking

within the Verie Walls of the College of Our Ladie and Saint Nicholas I have taken Steppes to Confronte the Evildoers with their Malefaction, the said Malefaction being Attested and Sworne to by Gilbert Fenton, Clerke, Elisabeth Shoemaker, Cook, and More Especially by Master Magnus Dobree, a Most Respect'd Member of our Facultie."

Now I must not conceal from you the fact that Sir John Cheke had only recently assumed his position as Provost; he had been appointed under a particular mandamus by Edward the Sixth, being neither a cleric, a doctor, nor a member of the foundation—three qualifications previously held to be essential. Neither had his elevation been entirely well received by those destined to serve under him: both the Vice-Provost and certain of his friends (amongst whom we have to number Master Magnus Dobree) being exceedingly reluctant to confirm their new Principal. However, rigid protocol and conscience alike tend to waver before the word of kings; Sir John had been appointed and had taken up office at the time of which we speak.

A period then of unease, of accusation, plot and counter-plot, when cruelty walked the land under a mask of reforming zeal and no man could hold himself entirely safe against the wagging of his neighbor's tongue. So it came about that two harmless, ineffective young men found themselves summoned to appear before the Provost and give a true and faithful account of their diabolic practices. As they had no diabolic practices other than a tendency to waste their time and that of their tutor by playing with marbles during his instruction, the note threw them into a state of some confusion.

"What's amiss?"

"You have some knowledge!"

"Not I!"

"Confess, you have visited Lolworth by stealth—?" (Lolworth being the village where the witch reputedly held sway.)

"As I hope to be saved, I would not venture within twenty miles of that accursed place—" And so on and so forth at great length until Chauncey Adam became persuaded that his friend Nicholas Palgrave really had no acquaintance with black sorcery, whereas

Nicholas for his part became disposed to acquit Chauncey Adam of any Satanic pretensions.

There remained the question, who had accused them? They sat late into the night searching their memory and could arrive at no satisfactory conclusion: they had the normal rivals amongst their fellow students, they had aggravated no more than the usual number of learned pedagogues by their persistent idleness. For my part I am afraid I can throw no light on the matter, other than to point out that numerous powerful academics were still eager to discredit Sir John and may—I make no positive assertion, I merely state an hypothesis—may have chosen our two at random simply as evidence of incompetence and misrule.

But if the identity of the accuser remained obscure, the accusations were very precise indeed. It had been alleged that no fewer than three witnesses had seen Master Palgrave and Master Adam returning at midnight down the Lolworth Road with blood on their hands and the feathers of a black cock adhering to their clothes; they looked, said the witness, "Most Strangely Alter'd, as Men Bereft of Freewyl."

Against such positive identification the students could only reply that they had been abed at the time—a statement which of necessity could not be proven. Sir John received them in his library. He spoke gravely of hell fire, he described the hideous torments of the damned and he urged them to renounce the Witch of Lolworth. As they did not know the Witch of Lolworth this presented certain insuperable difficulties. However, they swore most obligingly to have no further meeting with her whom they had never met and strained their imaginations to abjure opinions they had never had and ceremonies they had never seen.

Now I must not mislead you here; Sir John Cheke (John Cheke, as he was at the time) would appear to have been a most able and learned man, a humanist of some repute and a Greek scholar of renown. Whilst at St. John's, Cambridge, he had been Master of the Glomery: it is a matter of endless regret to me that I cannot tell you what the Glomery was or what the Master of it did—and neither can anyone else—the subject has defied the antiquaries. But Sir John was a man in all things to be respected, a convinced

Protestant and an ardent reformer. Unfortunately, at the period of which I speak, he had encountered difficulties at Court, he had been opposed by his colleagues and he found himself—as he wrote to a friend—"Much Toss'd by Storms and subject to Ambition's bitter Gall." Moreover, the affair of Mistress Norrys had become something more than a passing vexation. There had been a growing number of complaints relating to the Witch and her influence, and it behoved a prudent administrator to investigate.

The background to the story appears obscure, yet may have had its origin in the dissolution some ten years earlier of Poleworth Abbey. Poleworth had survived rather longer than most communities thanks to the efforts of the Commission, who reported that the Abbess Fitzherbert was "a very sadde Discrete and Relygous Woman who hath byn Heed and Governor these XXVII years." The Abbey should not be suppressed, said the Commissioners, for "the town of Poleworth wholy depends on the Nonnery and will be ruined by the suppression, and the people therin to the nombers of VI or VII score persons are Nott Unlikely to wander and to seke for their Lyvyng." The payment of fifty pounds secured the continuance of Poleworth, yet for only another ten years; then the Abbey suffered the same fate as the rest—it was dissolved, and no doubt the population did in truth "wander and seke for their Lyvyng." According to popular legend one of these unfortunates wandered as far afield as Lolworth, having on her long journey acquired certain black arts by which to survive. For, said the country folk, how could a helpless woman contrive to exist under such harsh conditions unless she were in league with the Devil? To which we may reply, how indeed? This, then, was the Witch of Lolworth, to whom Sir John Cheke gave such anxious thought.

He questioned Nicholas and Chauncey at some length, not from any malicious desire to persecute them, rather as a matter of concern touching the public safety. Faced with a string of palpable lies (for I am afraid the two boys lacked any subtlety in their defense) the Provost became irritable.

"Have a care, sirs. I am not to be mocked. When did you last have dealings with Mistress Norrys?"

"I misremember!"

" 'Tis long past, I swear."

"We never went to Lolworth—" And, simultaneously from Nicholas, "We shall never go back, on my oath!"

It continued in this garbled fashion. It is a melancholy fact that nothing sounds more guilty than the panic babblings of the confused innocent—particularly when there are two innocents who contradict each other at every turn. Sir John silenced them with a curt movement of his hand, demanding a full and penitent confession. They stammered miserably, again drowning in a sea of contradictions. His patience wore thin; he rose, declaring, "Here be witnesses to your malpractice. You have been observed upon your wicked errands a scant twelve hours ago!"

"Who has observed us?" cried Chauncey, quite taken aback by this new accusation. "You say that we were seen? By whom?"

"B-b-by me," said a thin voice, and Master Magnus Dobree slithered into the room, his gown rustling as he came. The boys had often mimicked the stutter and wild gestures of this dark, fanatical sort of man. When unable to control a hall full of students he would smite the desk and rush across the floor, often seizing one of his audience by the neck. A learned man, oh dear me yes—but unfortunate in his appearance and manner. He had a quite alarmingly narrow head, and sunken cheeks gave him the air of a galvanized cadaver. He had had hopes of advancement under the late Provost George Day—and still hoped for it under Sir John. Now he leant against the wall and eyed the pair unpleasantly.

They for their part began to utter more confused denials.

"This is not possible!"

"Would you call Master Dobree a liar?"

"Merely that he is mistaken in his belief."

"I think not." Dobree moved forward to give his superior a document, closely written in a crabbed hand. "We have a s-s-statement, given upon oath. The woman has confessed."

Confessed? Now here was a desperate situation indeed; the Witch of Lolworth had named Chauncey Adam and Nicholas Palgrave as her accomplices, her companions in the black art—and against her evidence there could be no appeal. Sir John spoke in grave sorrow, invoking help for their immortal souls; then he indicated that they were both dismissed from the college on which they had brought such shame. He would nevertheless exercise mercy, he would be lenient, he would do no more than order them on pain of imprisonment to leave Cambridge within the week.

They were under no illusion; given so black a reputation they stood in fearful danger; they would be fortunate to escape from the town without injury or, to speak plainly, with their lives. Chauncey and Nicholas sat by the river and debated their perilous case, Nicholas being for instant flight; but Chauncey (and I fancy he was the bolder of the two) dismissed the notion out of hand, for they could be waylaid on the road. No, their best hope, said he, lay in finding Mistress Norrys and forcing that malevolent creature to recant. They had innocence and youth on their side—surely the truth must prevail! It needed only to plead their case, to entreat the old woman to withdraw her monstrous charge, as surely she must when brought face to face with two boys she had never seen in her life yet bid fair to ruin. Courage might solve their dilemma—a bold confrontation with the witch herself. So argued Chauncey Adam, viciously throwing stones into the water. I do not say that Nicholas found himself in total agreement with the plan; I think it more probable he lacked the strength of character to oppose it. Be that as it may, Chauncey's determined logic overcame all obstacles. Waiting only for the cover of darkness the two friends wrapped themselves in warm cloaks and set off down the long road to Huntingdon.

A cold night with no moon. They spoke little, being altogether too cast down and melancholy. They trudged on beside the hedgerows, exchanging the barest of remarks—a word of warning as they encountered a wide ditch, a brief consultation when they came to a milestone. About midnight they discovered the side-turning which must take them to Lolworth; and here the track grew narrower, the bushes more obtrusive; there had been rain earlier in the day and horseriders had churned the path into a quagmire.

I have said there was no moon; for which reason the appearance of a distant light puzzled them. They paused, fearing some unlucky encounter. As they watched, the light split into various parts and presently showed itself to be a line of flickering points—in brief, a procession of torches. What this might be neither man could determine; what struck both of them with an alarming certainty was the realization that should it continue on its present course they would of necessity meet the procession face to face—a most undesirable prospect. The lane admitted of no side escape; they were perhaps half a mile from the crossroads. The line of light came steadily forward and now they could hear the distant noise of chanting voices. Acting on a joint impulse the young men scrambled through the hedge and flung themselves flat on the ground; to run across open fields would invite detection, to lie still could just save them. Chauncey threw his cloak over his head, urging Nicholas to do the same—and still the night walkers came nearer. The glow from their flambeaux turned the bushes to scarlet, shadows elongated themselves across the grass and the chant formed into recognizable words.

"We triumph! Satan is put to flight! The righteous shall prevail forever!"

Nicholas raised his head the better to peer between the branches; and what he saw caused him to grasp Chauncey by the arm.

"Hush!"

"Chauncey, but look—"

"Hush!"

Some twenty people passed between the hedgerows singing and shouting with great vigor; their shadows capered at their heels, foreshortened into grotesque blobs. Then they came to a bend in the path and were seen no more, though for several minutes the sound of their voices could be heard while pinpoints of flame flashed across the countryside.

Nicholas rose to his feet in stark astonishment, crying softly to his friend, "Did you not see him—? Did you not *see*?" Chauncey nodded; for he too had recognized the lean body of Magnus Dobree leaping at the head of the procession. They turned their backs on this inexplicable cavalcade and walked on towards Lolworth, debating at some length what it could signify.

They arrived in the village before daybreak to spend the remainder of the night sleeping comfortably enough against a hayrick. A wandering cockerel woke them. After much anxious discussion they fetched a wide circuit round the hamlet and so encountered a farm laborer on the outskirts of the place.

Idle conversation. Remarks as casual as the two students could make them.

"A fine day."

"Aye, 'tis."

"The village yonder—Lolworth, perhaps?"

"Aye, 'tis."

"You live there, perchance?"

"Aye, that I do, sir."

Now for the danger point, the moment when Chauncey must of necessity put the question direct. "You are acquainted with a woman—oh, I misremember her name. Aid me, Nicholas, what is her name?"

"Mistress Norrys," muttered Nicholas, and saw the countryman's eyes narrow and feared that they had ruined all. Fool! to have been so hasty, to show their purpose altogether too plain. The silence lengthened whilst high above them in the morning sky a bird cried once.

The fellow gazed at them with a most disquieting intensity. Finally he threw down his pitchfork saying, "Why d'you ask?"

"We would speak with her," replied Chauncey, who believed very sensibly that boldness held the key to safety.

"Speech? You would have speech with her? You would have *speech*?" Suddenly, disconcertingly, the laborer began to laugh; he leant against the hayrick and gave way to a horrid kind of bubbling mirth which caused his eyes to water and his mouth to dribble. At last, wiping both mouth and eyes with the back of his sleeve, he gained sufficient control of himself to gasp, "Nay, nay! You're altogether too late, young sir."

"Has she gone?" cried Chauncey, seized with a dreadful premonition.

"Gone? Nay, she's not *gone*. Nor will go now by any road, I fancy! She's six feet underground."

They questioned him at that, and beyond doubt it was so. Mistress Norrys, the Witch of Lolworth, had been hanged the night before—by the very mob they had encountered capering down the lane in savage triumph; tried, hanged, and her body thrown into an old gravel pit far beyond the village. Their accuser was dead—the only witness whose word might have saved them.

Chauncey and Nicholas walked slowly out into the country and were most horribly afraid. As the day grew older they wore themselves into exhaustion with talk, searching desperately for a remedy, and it may well have been the hopelessness of that task which caused them to walk in circles, eventually drawing them back into Lolworth so that noon found them standing outside the cottage where the Witch had lived. In their fury the mob had burnt the house too; nothing remained except blackened walls (the thatch being entirely destroyed), a few broken pieces of some poor furniture and a little smoke which still drifted up into the sky. I do not know what perverse inclination made them enter the place, neither can I tell you what they hoped to find—unless desperate imagining made them believe they could lay their hands on evidence, any kind of evidence, to clear themselves. They certainly subjected the ruins to a very close scrutiny. It was, I think, Chauncey who peered up the blackened chimney-stack, and in so doing dislodged a quantity of dusty bricks which clattered to the ground bringing with them a small metal box.

It had retained the heat to a surprising degree, being still quite difficult to handle several hours after the fire. Nicholas held it firm whilst Chauncey went to work on it with his dagger. Both lock and hinges had become sadly distorted, making the operation hard and tedious—yet it yielded in the end. Chauncey prised back the lid to reveal a small leatherbound volume.

A curious heat lingered about that too. The parchment had not been scorched, yet the book gave off a distinct smell of burning; the result, possibly, of smoke which must have poured up the chimney. They bent over their find. The lettering seemed ancient, the text written in a crabbed hand in a kind of dog-Latin horribly awkward to follow, almost incomprehensible. There were illustrations too of a most unsavory kind, designs, strange fragments of verse, and a drawing of a creature with horns and the face of a reptile, which caused poor Nicholas to start and glance over his shoulder.

Now, it must be emphasized that these two young men knew nothing at all about witchcraft, their preoccupations being the normal ones for their age—that is to say, wine, the society of young ladies, and the avoidance of as many of their lectures as could safely be missed. They were blessed with only moderate intelligence and a rather limited curiosity—average, you see: two pleasant, commonplace, average students. Until Master Dobree denounced them, until Sir John Cheke spoke so gravely and dismissed them from their studies, they had heard of the Witch of Lolworth only as a name mentioned in idle tavern gossip. Yet here they stood in the ruins of her cottage examining what could only be her handbook.

A growing fascination held them. They read on, translating as best they could, correcting each other, repeating ancient rhymes, Latin tags and old Egyptian sorceries. The walls cooled as the hours went by, smoke no longer drifted up from the charred floor. Chauncey drew strange diagrams in the ashes with the point of his dagger and stared curiously at the result.

I do not know why they spoke in whispers.

"Can such things be?"

"As a Christian I hold myself bound to deny it!"

"Yet here in the village they called her Witch!"

"A harmless crone."

"Then why hang her, answer me that, why was she hanged—unless they had good reason to be afraid?"

They gazed at each other and neither could supply a rational answer, an explanation calculated to ease their feverish minds; yet as they squatted on the ground certain dark possibilities became apparent. For if the dead Mistress Norrys had indeed been a witch possessed of weird demoniacal powers, might not these same powers be put to an entirely different end and used to help the living? In a word, to save the lives of Master Nicholas Palgrave and his good friend Master Chauncey Adam? They did not come light-ly upon any such conclusion. They eyed each other slantwise as though hazarding a guess, each boy attempting to measure the lengths to which his companion might go. They continued to talk in a nervous undertone.

"Would you endanger your immortal soul?"

"There is no choice!"

"To traffic with the Devil is a grievous sin!"

"Mark me well, lest we have means to our defense we are but dead men—"

So they argued, with Chauncey ever the stronger and more persuasive till in the end he had quite won over Nicholas, had got him to agree that if—I say, if—the dusty volume yielded a suitable incantation, a proven way of ridding oneself of dangerous enemies, it would be no more than sensible to employ it against Master Magnus Dobree. Much of the work seemed incomprehensible, curious yet malevolent words. There were pictures of such horror that Nicholas moved on hurriedly and would not turn the page back.

Night found them crouched amongst the ruins with their treasure, still undecided as to the meaning of the thing; then by common consent they set out across the darkening fields to discover the Witch's burial place.

The gravel pit proved to be a good three miles distant from Lolworth, a gaping hole back against the deeper blackness of the land. They held close to each other for comfort and support, the ground being perilously uneven. I cannot tell what prompted them to such a desperate adventure other than mortal dread and a mounting frustration at their inability to understand even one word of the manuscript. They were possessed of a fierce desire to wring some meaning from the spidery writing, even if they had to drag Mistress Norrys from her grave to interpret the script.

As they drew near, Nicholas became increasingly agitated, but Chauncey broke away, advancing boldly to the very edge of the chasm. He stared down—and then leapt aside, catching at his breath. Two eyes were looking back at him.

The gasp of terror brought Nicholas hurrying forward. He in his turn peered into the pit and saw a Thing squatting on the loose earth, a formless blob of hair which resembled nothing either animal or human yet had in the center two small squinting eyes.

I have said that Nicholas Palgrave lacked the courage of his friend. He gave one wild shriek and fled across the fields, frightening the night birds who shot up startled from their resting-places in the trees. Chauncey ran after him, still clutching the book; and neither man stopped running till they were halfway down the road that led them back to Cambridge.

"A God's name, what was it?"

"Some fiend from hell!"

"We have been meddling with dangerous sorceries! I beseech you, throw the book away!"

"Not I," said Chauncey, and he slackened his pace. "I hold fast to our only hope of salvation." Then he gripped the volume more firmly under his arm. "Come, we are not children to start at every jack rabbit!"

He walked on, leaving Nicholas to trail unhappily behind him crying, "It was not a rabbit, Chauncey! It was not a rabbit!"

For several miles neither boy spoke. Unlike the previous evening a full moon presently appeared, flooding the landscape with cold light; this time they met no procession or indeed any living soul. Nicholas attempted to whistle and abandoned the tuneless effort. Chauncey muttered to himself, repeating strange words and phrases from the Witch of Lolworth's manuscript, rolling the syllables and pondering on their meaning. They continued in this manner for an hour or so while the moon shone and the hedges slipped past them; then Nicholas became aware of a distant humming noise, a buzzing in the air.

"Chauncey! Hold!"

"What now?"

"Can you not *hear*?"

"Nothing."

"Listen, I pray you, listen—"

Now both men heard it, a sound of innumerable insects steadily growing closer; and now they saw it, a cloud approaching down the empty road, rising and falling as it came. It looked more curious than alarming. No doubt you have seen a dozen midges dancing of a summer's evening; well, save for the fact that they could be numbered in thousands rather than dozens, these creatures produced the same effect—a mass of infinitely small particles lifting and dropping, lifting and dropping. Our students paused to gaze back at them, puzzled to observe such a thing at a late hour when most of Nature slept. They were not sufficiently knowledgeable to say whether the phenomenon were usual, yet grew most powerfully persuaded that it was *unnatural*.

They lingered too long staring at the flies. By the time they turned to continue their journey the swarm had caught up with them. Chauncey and Nicholas became enveloped in a buzzing cloud which smelt abominable and covered them from head to toe with crawling, stinging, heaving bodies. Nicholas gave a shout and took to his heels; Chauncey grabbed a stick from the hedgerow and began to belabor the surrounding air in a vain attempt to keep the attack at bay—as well as try to fight off the wind with blows. The tiny insects disintegrated when he touched them, and for every one that vanished four more materialized. Abandoning the hopeless task he threw the stick away and joined his friend in pell-mell flight.

I cannot tell what might have been the end of this unpleasant business, certainly neither Chauncey nor Nicholas could run fast enough to outdistance the pursuing wings. As chance would have it, however, they rounded a bend in the path to find themselves skirting a river-bank. Both men leapt into the water yelling. When they surfaced the road lay deserted and nothing troubled the air but a faint breeze.

So it came about that they arrived in Cambridge at four in the morning, exhausted and dripping wet. They put on dry clothes, and commenced packing with some urgency, for the sooner they left the town behind the better it would be for them. A bare half-hour saw them on the road again. Whilst passing the college gates Chauncey took his companion by the arm.

"Stay a moment."

"What now?"

"We have a small matter of business to transact."

"You surely would not dare—"

"I would not leave the enemy to persecute us as he chose!"

Now twin horrors took hold of Nicholas Palgrave: a superstitious dread of actually using witchcraft, and a much more immediate fear of the consequences to themselves should Master Magnus Dobree follow up his accusations—possibly by means of dispatches sent to London.

Dawn had scarcely begun to outline the university buildings as they stood at the doorway of his chambers debating furiously in whispers.

"This is black sacrilege!"

"He would burn us, given due cause and opportunity!"

"Let us rather appeal to the king."

"Against Magnus Dobree—? Oh, oh, oh! and what's a king? Master Buchanan would say the late King Henry used to burn men of opposing beliefs in the same bonfire if it suited his purpose."

"I have no faith in magic incantations, Chauncey!"

"Then it matters not what we do!"

So they argued, and as ever Chauncey proved the more powerful advocate. He took the leather volume from inside his cloak. Thumbing the pages he came upon certain words writ large in Latin. I regret that I cannot tell you what they may have been, and if I could would hesitate to do so. He recited them carefully and with a particular emphasis; then he threw the book in at Magnus Dobree's window and they fled.

At this point I must rely again on Sir John Cheke, who wrote to his friend Sir William Butts of Thornage as follows:

"A Most Horrid Tragedie has been Enacted here. Master Magnus Dobree—concerning whom I have had Occasion to speke—was Dicover'd Dead in hys chambers on St. Philip's Daie. Hys servant, on Discoverying the Bodie, did come to me in much alarm: and for my part I cannot Blame the Fellow. Master Dobree, as I presentlie Perceiv'd for myself, did lie most Naturallie in hys Bedde; yet hys Bodie had Swollen to a Monstrous Size and Seem'd entirely covered in Boils. Moreover, the chamber itself was Full of Flyes, which have not to this Daie been Dislodg'd."

So wrote Sir John Cheke, in considerable perplexity. As for Chauncey Adam and Nicholas Palgrave, why, they vanished down the London road and appear no more in this history. For myself I can merely conclude that it is not wise to accuse innocent and perhaps rather simple men of witchcraft, for you may turn their minds to matters which otherwise would never have concerned them.

Sheila Hodgson started in the theater and then joined the B.B.C. as a staff writer. She has many radio and television plays to her credit. She now works as a free lance and has had two stage plays produced and a novel published. "The Turning Point" was inspired by M.R. James' essay, at the end of his Collected Ghost Stories, *in which he lists short notes for the use of other writers. Sheila Hodgson has also adapted the work of Algernon Blackwood and Friedrich Dürrenmatt.*

"The creation of a mood of false confidence, he felt, was something that could best be left to the newspapers."

The Conference

BY ERNO PAASILINNA

Withering sarcasm in a fast-paced political satire.

DR. Smith said that he did not believe that any immediate threat of an invasion from Space was likely to arise for some time. Observations to date had given no support to the view that any such preparations had been put in hand. Technically they were of course ahead of us, but in his opinion there was no cause for panic. Nor could he endorse the widespread but naive assumption that any confrontation with beings from Space must inevitably lead to war. If human beings had reason to feel threatened, it was from each other that the chief threat came. He urged the Conference to work for a situation in which every country would be preparing for peace rather than for war. He said he had no wish to sound sardonic, but that he had noticed that when war was prepared for, it was usually war that ensued.

Dr. Smith pointed out that in the course of their reconnaissance missions the Spatials had behaved with the utmost discretion and had avoided any kind of aggressive behavior towards human beings. Much had been said about the Barcelona incident, in which the driver of a car was killed, but in Dr. Smith's opinion this was a case of simple self-defense, and any pilot in such an emergency might have acted in the same way. The driver had approached the unknown aviator in a threatening manner, pointing a weapon at him and ordering him to put up his hands. The fate of the three hikers captured near Dublin was, he agreed, a different matter, but he felt sure this incident could be explained as an operation motivated by scientific curiosity. There was no evidence that the humans concerned were subjected to torture or to any other kind of personal indignity.

According to eye-witness accounts they were simply led into the spacecraft, which then took off. The impression Dr. Smith had gained from these reports was that, far from being kidnapped, the hikers had accompanied the visitors voluntarily. One of them was said to have laughed and waved his hand. Viewed in the light of the present situation on Earth, this hiker's behavior struck him as not at all unreasonable, and might well have been intended as a deliberate gesture. It was natural that the Spatials should have an interest in the study of human physiology and behavior. This aspect of the question was one to which he hoped particular attention would be paid by the distinguished members of the present Conference.

A delegate from the United States said that he could not associate himself with the views expressed by the previous speaker. The creation of a mood of false confidence, he felt, was something that could best be left to the newspapers: governments would do better to pay attention to the dangerous security situation into which they appeared to have drifted. The likelihood of an armed invasion was borne out by the frequency with which sightings had occurred in the vicinity of research stations and military installations. "Our good friend Dr. Smith," he added, "must surely be aware of these sightings. Information collated in Western countries alone shows that the Spatials are aware of every one of our projects, however marginal in importance. The atomic submarine *Tornado*, which disappeared during the Pacific manoeuvres last year, was literally snatched from under our very noses. I would like to inform Dr. Smith that many of the military experts attending this conference would welcome the return of that submarine. Perhaps Dr. Smith could make the necessary arrangements? And it is no good saying that the disappearance of our most valuable nuclear submarine is not an established fact: several admirals of the U.S. Navy and a large number of other naval officers are witnesses to the fact that the submarine, while actually taking part in an exercise, was lifted bodily from the water and conveyed into an immense flying ship, which then vanished. I have no wish to pour scorn on Dr. Smith's innocent optimism, and I am perfectly ready to agree that this provocative action against the United States be described as motivated by scientific interest: I only wish I could feel as happy about this as he does."

To this Dr. Smith replied that he had no wish to deny that the events reported had actually happened. But he did wish members of the Conference to appreciate the possibility that the Spatials might be interested in our technological products merely as quaint curiosities. This seemed to be borne out by the fact that they had not destroyed them but had set out to obtain a representative specimen. In this they appeared to have succeeded.

A general from the U.S.S.R. said that perhaps he failed to appreciate an ironical intention behind the remarks of Dr. Smith. He asked whether Dr. Smith was the representative of any particular government. Dr. Smith replied that he was not. The general asked him whom, in that case, he did think he was representing; was it perhaps the Spatials themselves? Dr. Smith stated that he was attending the Conference at the invitation of the organizers, as an independent expert. The Spatials hardly needed a defense counsel at the present Conference, he added; if anything, the boot was on the other foot.

Turning to the organizers, the general proposed that Dr. Smith's expert opinion be now taken as heard, and discussion be resumed on the basis of military questions. He said that it might have been more helpful to the work of the Conference if Dr. Smith's report had dealt with matters more relevant to the realities of the situation.

Dr. Smith having left the hall, the general expressed his regret at the losses suffered by the United States, and said that the Soviet Union had known about these. He said he considered it significant that the interest of the Spatials now seemed to be so firmly concentrated on military activities. We should perhaps start from the assumption that our existing inventions are known to them, and that there is not much chance of our concealing any from them in the future. He thought it a pity that in estimating the balance of military power we had so little to go by. A number of metal objects had been picked up, but the study of these had been held up by the unfamiliarity of the material: in the almost complete absence of any known point of reference, analysis had proved diffcult. But this, said the general, was still only one side of the question. Once people began to question whether there was any point in continuing defense preparations, the war would be as good as lost. Looking back over the debate so far, he could say that the Soviet Union, at any rate, had made its position plain. He referred to the similar stand taken by the U.S. government, and hoped that other governments would follow suit. What was at stake was the fate of the entire human race.

A speaker from the floor suggested that it might be worth-while considering for what ultimate purpose the conquest of Earth might be regarded by the Spatials as necessary. He said that this question should not be thought of simply in terms of traditional strategic objectives. If he might himself put forward a suggestion, was it not possible that there might be a nutritional aspect? If it were established that Earth had anything to offer the Spatials in that respect, then an armed invasion might well be a possibility.

A biologist from Kenya expressed doubts as to whether, the Earth's own nutritional situation being what it is, the Spatials would content themselves with the limited advantages to be gained from an occupation *per se*. The results would certainly not justify the sacrifices involved in the operation. If the Spatials' objective was purely and simply to improve their own food supply, he saw little hope that the Earth's original inhabitants would be capable of surviving. It was of course possible that the organic products of the Earth could be adapted to the nutritional requirements of spatial beings, but it was equally possible that their principal interest would be focused on the human species itself. He warned his hearers, however, not to infer from these remarks that he was himself in any sense advocating the utilization of Man as a source of nutriment for the Spatials.

The Belgian delegate said that the view just propounded was an interesting one, and might well prove to be correct. He suggested that it might be worth-while to consider to what extent Man could be put to use by the Spatials as a source of food, for example by intensive stock improvement and processing. We would then know what advantages they might hope to gain. He said that it would be unwise to predict such a development, but that if it did become inevitable it would be as well to have made some preparations in advance. A certain repugnance might be felt for the idea of such a system, but this should not prevent us from discussing the problem on a theoretical level. Personally he believed that very high production figures could be achieved. This would involve maintaining the greater part of mankind in zoos, utilizing the Earth's own food resources for the purpose. In this way a considerable increase in the human population could be guaranteed. He reckoned that by strict and equal rationing, under carefully regulated conditions, it would be possible to breed for production purposes some 16—18 billion individuals—a figure not far short of the kind of target that might be expected to interest the Spatials. Under the existing system, said the Belgian delegate, the rationing of food was carried out very unevenly, a fact which had given rise to criticism in some quarters.

The Norwegian delegate asked whether the turn now taken by the debate meant that the Conference was abandoning the discussion of possible military solutions, and was going to concentrate on the type of solution now put forward. He said that he had no authority from his government to take part in any discussion of that kind. If he had rightly understood the proposal, it involved an unconditional surrender on the part of the human race.

A U.S. delegate replied that the two problems should not be regarded as separate: both formed part of the overall military picture. By analyzing the probable aims of the Spatials, one could also determine what problems would have to be faced in the event of the failure of military measures. It was not necessary to think purely in terms of a surrender: to put it more tactfully, some kind of compromise might well be possible.

The next speaker was a Swiss expert, who said that as a scientist he was naturally not qualified to give any opinion on the military side of the question, but that he felt that speakers so far had been tending to take it for granted that human meat possessed a higher nutritional value than animal meat. This, of course, was largely a matter of taste, and the question could perhaps be left aside for the moment. It was, however, undoubtedly true that human beings were very much more suitable than animals for breeding in large quantities. In his view, that part of the human race possessing a higher level of intellect could be trained as keepers and put in charge of the human beings earmarked for purposes of meat production. In this way the need for occupation forces would be greatly reduced, and more attention could be paid to animal breeding. There was no reason to suppose, he pointed out, that the breeding of animals could not be carried on side by side with that of humans. These were purely practical considerations, he said in conclusion.

A French delegate stated that in the case of human beings a considerable degree of stock improvement could certainly be effected: the average *per capita* carcass weight could be increased and the quality of the meat improved to suit requirements. Such calculations might sound somewhat macabre, but these were after all simple biological facts. He thought that the human beings trained as keepers might also be made responsible for quality control and grading, while their specialized knowledge of conditions on Earth would enable them to act as expert advisers. He thought there were excellent chances for co-operation along these lines. On the ethical side of the question he preferred not to commit himself to an opinion, as this was clearly a matter on which a specialist should be consulted.

A delegate rose to point out that no consideration had yet been given to the fact that the distribution and storage of human carcasses in such massive quantities might involve considerable problems. He said that while he believed production on an industrial scale to be perfectly feasible under earthly conditions, the possibility of interplanetary marketing was still a matter of pure speculation. The conversion of Earth into a kind of food repository for the use of Space would still, in his opinion, depend upon the solution of a number of detailed problems, although, of course, this was not to say that such solutions would not be found.

A professor from West Germany said that although he had not originally intended to speak in the debate, he was now moved to do so because, in his opinion, an offer on the part of responsible representatives of the Earth to organize and co-ordinate a meat supply would be just the kind of voluntary gesture that would most probably be expected of them by the occupying power. The creation of a supervisory body for this purpose seemed to him an excellent idea. He believed that the Spatials would be anxious to keep down the cost of meat production, while at the same time avoiding too great a commitment of personnel to duties on this planet. The professor considered that in the event of an invasion it would be important for the Spatials to know whether there were people on the Earth capable of directing operations and developing production. He did not wish to seem ultra-patriotic, but perhaps his own country could claim to offer a certain amount of useful experience in this connection. He proposed the immediate establishment of a high-level Commission, which could carry out the necessary preliminary arrangements and prepare the ground for contacts with the Spatials. He would leave open the question as to what detailed arrangements would be involved, but he certainly considered that the preliminary steps should be taken as a matter of urgency.

Born 1935 near Petsamo (now Pechenga) on the Arctic coast, Erno Paasilinna and his family were evacuated during World War II upheavals and forced to lead a nomadic life as refugees. He completed his education and started to write in Northern Finland. He was editor of Pohjoinen, *a periodical which became a thorn to the establishment. From 1966 to 1971 he worked for the publishing house Karisto, becoming the chief literary editor. Since then he has been working as a free-lance writer. In addition to fiction, his output in newspaper columns, television, articles and essays is impressive. His concern for the world is frequently expressed in grim satire. Mr. Paasilinna has been honored with several awards for his work. "The Conference" was translated by David Barrett.*

"If I have any chance at all,
it is by doing the one thing the Germans
do not expect me to do: to walk straight to them."

Thank You, Dr. Coué

BY ROBERT MULLER

The author, a world statesman and practicing optimist, shares a daring escape.

WHEN I studied at the University of Heidelberg during the war, I lodged in a boardinghouse located in the Hauptstrasse near the Karlstor. Students from several occupied countries resided there, together with Germans who were allowed to study because they had been wounded or because they were needed as doctors or technicians in Hitler's army.

In a room next to mine, on the top floor of the building, lived a Yugoslav named Slavko Bosnjakovich. He was a tall, soft-spoken, aristocratic young man, endowed with the finest features. Despite his youth—he was twenty-seven years old—he had been a colonel in the Yugoslav army. Released from German prison camp, he had come to Heidelberg to study law. His intelligent face carried a dreamy and superior quality, intermingled with considerable strength drawn from his hawklike nose. His complexion was very pale, almost transparent, and his light gray eyes gave him at times a rather distant appearance. We were great friends and became very fond of each other. We were both dreamers and full of expectations about life. I liked his distinguished calm outlook and intelligence, and he my animal-like passion for life and my carefree, wild behavior and laughter. We spent innumerable hours together, either in his room or in mine, discussing life, death, and the future of the world. To this day, I can recall the fragrance of his long, blond Serbian cigarettes, which he smoked from the edge of his lips as if they were a rare, prohibited delicacy.

During the winter of 1942, I wanted to invite him to our home in Lorraine for Christmas, but I knew that my parents, who were living in a rather secluded fashion, would not endorse my invitation. So I abandoned the idea and went home alone. When I returned to Heidelberg in early January our landlady greeted me with sad news:

"Your poor friend is severely ill. A few days ago I found him lying on the floor of his room, unconscious, with blood spilling from his mouth. I called a doctor, and an ambulance took him to the hospital. They fear the worst for him. Apparently he is suffering from a very advanced case of tuberculosis."

I rushed to the hospital, where I found my dear friend lying propped up in bed, leaning against a pile of white cushions. He was thinner and paler than ever. The skin of his face was moist, sickly, yellow like wax. His long, thin hands were lifeless and almost transparent. He was breathing softly and carefully, as if not to unduly tax his poor lungs. But in the midst of this image of desolation, his eyes were glowing with happiness when he saw me. His attitude of calm superiority had not abandoned him. He tried to reassure me about his condition, while in my mind I could not help visualizing the ravages that reigned in his narrow, concave chest.

I was allowed to stay with him for an hour or so. When I took leave, he asked me for a favor:

"Could you please go to the university library and borrow for me any books you can find written by a certain Dr. Coué or by his disciples? Bring them to me as soon as possible."

I went there the following morning and found indeed a book by

Dr. Émile Coué entitled *Self-mastery Through Conscious Auto-suggestion*, as well as a book written about him by one of his disciples. I thus learned that a doctor from my neighboring town of Nancy in Lorraine had gained worldwide fame for his healing methods based on the confidence and imagination of the patient. In the 1920s he attracted enormous audiences in England and in the United States, where he produced many miraculous cures with his psychological method. His disciple, whose name I have forgotten, had broadened Dr. Coué's views into a philosophy, in which self-confidence, good health, and happiness were the cornerstones of life. I absorbed the contents of the two books in a few hours before bringing them to my friend. To this day I have not forgotten their theme:

Every morning before rising, and every evening on getting into bed, shut your eyes and repeat several times: "Every day, in every way, I am getting better and better." One can add one's own words, and I got accustomed to saying: I feel wonderful, I feel happier than yesterday, I have never felt so good, it is marvelous to be alive and so healthy, etc.

The remainder of the two books were merely elaborations of this central theme. I thought at first that it was a little easy to seek happiness by just repeating to oneself that one felt happy! There was no depth in such a philosophy. But after reflection I agreed that man had indeed the choice of seeing everything in light or in dark and that it was not unwise to start the day with the conviction that one felt good, healthy, and happy to be alive. The amount and intensity of happiness, one's zest for life, one's attitude toward the surrounding world are perhaps determined after all by a basic "internal" decision taken at the beginning of the day.

I brought the books to my friend who, to the great surprise of the doctors, recovered within a few weeks and was released from the hospital.

I have never forgotten Slavko Bosnjakovich and Dr. Coué's method. True enough, as with prayers, I have not always repeated the suggested daily words, but I have instinctively followed Dr. Coué's philosophy of optimism and self-reliance all my life. Many times at the United Nations, when bad news tends to drag me down, I revert to an innermost part of myself, switch on optimism and confidence, and immediately I return to a positive, creative mood. This mysterious quantum change between a negative and a positive current in the total functioning of the human being is the great lesson I have learned from Dr. Coué and Slavko Bosnjakovich. It is a mystery to me. I do not understand it. But it has done miracles for me and it certainly saved my life on at least one if not on several occasions during the war, as the following story will illustrate.

After a series of adventures and an arrest by the Gestapo, I was finally able to cross the border between Germany and France in the summer of 1943. I was working under the false identity of Louis Parizot in a French telecommunications center located in Vichy. In that center, radio messages were recorded that provided the French Government with intelligence information and political news from the rest of the world. It was an ideal situation to infiltrate with members of the Resistance. Several draft evaders from Alsace-Lorraine had found refuge and a job in it. I got an administrative position that enabled me to warn my friends in the technical center, located in the woods outside the city, of impending inspections by the Germans. Their visits had to receive the prior consent of the French authorities, and I was able to obtain complete information.

I had been working there for a few months when one evening, in my hotel room, I noticed that someone had gone through my possessions. It was almost imperceptible, but I had the feeling that there was something wrong, and I asked the hotelkeeper if anyone had entered my room. "Yes, two workers from the electrical company checked it." I could not know whether it had been a routine inspection by the French police, or if the Germans were on my trail, or if electrical workers had indeed displaced some of my belongings.

The following morning I was sitting in my office when I received a telephone call from the guard at the entrance of the building. Like most French governmental services in Vichy, ours was located in a former hotel, in this case the Hotel de Grignan. The guard told me that three gentlemen wanted to see me on behalf of a friend named André Royer. I asked him to have them wait for a while and then let them come to my office on the second floor. My heart had jumped violently when I heard the name of André Royer, for the news had just reached me that this good schoolfriend of mine from my hometown in Lorraine had been arrested by the Germans during a raid on the University of Strasbourg and evacuated to the city of Clermont-Ferrand. The men who were on their way to my office were possibly Germans. I told my secretary to receive them, to find out what they wanted, and to let me know by telephoning the secretary of a colleague in a nearby office where I took refuge.

After a while the telephone rang and I heard my secretary say to the other girl:

"'I am looking for Mr. Parizot. Do you know where he is? Three gentlemen from the police want to see him."

This message was clear enough. When the phone hung up, I heard loud shouting. A man with a heavy German accent was screaming at my secretary:

"*Si fou ne me tites pas ou est Parizot che fou fais fousiller.*" (If you do not tell me where Parizot is, I will have you shot.)

To gain time for thought, I decided to proceed to the hotel's attics, and I asked the secretary who had harbored me to give a message to one of my colleagues who was a member of the Resistance. He joined me soon thereafter and gave me the following report:

"You have little chance of escape, if any. There are five or six Gestapos in the building. They are systematically searching offices and appear quite relaxed, for they know that you are here. The entrance to the hotel is blocked and a prison van is stationed at the curb. To hide here in the attics or climb on the roof will not help. You know perfectly well that that they will shoot you down like a pigeon."

He left me after these cheerful words, promising to return if there were any new developments, and I found myself alone to consider the trap I was in:

"This is the moment of all moments," I thought to myself, "to keep cool and in full command of my mental and physical capabilities." I suddenly remembered Dr. Coué. "I must feel relaxed and even elated about this situation." Following the good doctor's advice, I repeated to myself that it was indeed an extraordinary and thrilling adventure for a twenty-year-old youth to be trapped in a hotel, pursued by the Nazis. Would it not be exciting if I could play a trick on them and slip through their fingers?

Having thus switched my persepctive to a positive, confident frame of mind, I felt relaxed, even happy and cheerful, without any fear or thought of failure whatever.

I began to think calmly and decisively. My sequence of thoughts was as follows: "Nothing is hopeless in this world. There must be at least one chance in a thousand to escape from this situation. I must find it, and for that, I must concentrate on the mentality of the Nazis. They know that I am in this building. They are several. They have guarded the entrance. They are convinced that they will get me and that it is only a matter of time and *Gründlichkeit* (thoroughness). There is no classical means of escape. I must think of something that would be foreign to their psychology."

I let my thoughts wander in this direction and examined various options, of which all but one led to certain arrest and possible death. A little flicker of hope arose in the following suggestion:

"There are many people in the hotel. My best chance of escape is to become part of the crowd. Why not walk downstairs and go straight to the group of people who must be gathered on my floor? The Nazis certainly do not expect me to do that. The worst that could happen would be to be arrested. But this is likely to happen anyway. If I have any chance at all, it is by doing the one thing the Germans do not expect me to do: walk straight to them."

I put my plan immediately into action. I changed my physical appearance as best as I could, wetting my hair with water from a faucet in one of the former maids' rooms, and parting it on the side. I took off my glasses and lit a cigarette to gain a relaxed posture. Once on the fourth floor I seized a file from a desk and placed it under my arm. On the third floor I caught a glimpse of two Germans who were inspecting offices, but there was no disquietude. It seemed that few people knew what was going on. But it was a different story when I walked down the majestic staircase from the third to the second floor.

A large gathering of people had assembled, mostly officials who had been asked to vacate their offices. I could not see very well without my glasses, but nevertheless I was able to distinguish a group dominated by shiny spots: These must be the bald heads of the Germans, I surmised, and I decided to walk straight up to them. An infinitesimal fraction of silence set in when my French colleagues saw me appear on the staircase, but they immediately understood what I was trying to do, and they chatted louder than before in order to create a diversion. I walked up to the group of Germans and recognized my secretary, whom they were still interrogating. I asked her calmly:

"What is all this turmoil about?"

She answered very composedly:

"These gentlemen are looking for Mr. Parizot."

I expressed surprise:

"Parizot? But I just saw him a few minutes ago on the fourth floor!"

"*Schnell hinauf!*" (Quickly upstairs!) shouted one of the Germans, and the whole group moved into action and ran upstairs!

I maneuvered casually for a few more minutes, in case I was being observed by one of the smarter Nazis. My French colleagues were careful not to pay any attention to me, and they returned to their desks. I went to the office of a compatriot, Dieffenbacher, from my hometown, and asked him how I could get out of the building.

"The main entrance is guarded, but there may be a way of getting to the garage through the cellars. The French superintendent downstairs should be able to help you."

I walked down to the entrance lobby and talked to the *concierge*. There was indeed an exit through the cellars, and he led me to it. Midway he suddenly took fright, thinking of the possible reprisals by the Germans. I persuaded him to help me and, under his guidance, I finally reached the garage, which was full of bicycles. I took a good, sturdy one and rode to the house of a former French officer who was a member of the underground. There I waited for a few days until the search had abated and then proceeded to St. Étienne in the Auvergne, where I joined an active *maquis* in the hills.

I learned later that the Germans had been so thorough and convinced of finding me that they had even unrolled old carpets stored in the attics!

After the war, I met again with my secretary, Madeleine Grange, who told me that when I walked down the staircase, she was reciting to herself:

"Passera, passera pas, passera, etc. . . ." (Will pass, will not pass, will pass, etc. . . .)

I also learned from her that the Gestapo had a picture of me, a detail that I fortunately did not know, for if I had, it is possible that even Dr. Coué's method would not have helped me.

Ever since, and after several other instances when Dr. Coué's method saved me from very difficult situations during the war, no one has ever been able to convince me that optimism is not preferable to pessimism. Truly, my optimism has often been challenged and resented as being contrary to the prevailing rules of life, but I have never been given a solid reason to join the other side. The complexity of world affairs demands that those who deal with them be confident and strive to do their utmost even in the face of greatest difficulties. The sad chorus of pessimists only makes matters worse. To be a human is to live on the positive and sunny side of life that God has given us. Optimism, hard work, and faith are not only in our highest self-interest, they are also the affirmations of life itself. To give up, to see only hurdles and dead ends ahead is not the right attitude toward the great privilege of life. I was fortunate that one of my compatriots from the wartorn borderland of Alsace-Lorraine taught me this at an early age. It is perhaps in regions that have suffered the most that people acquire extra reasons to hope and an iron will to cope with the obstacles presented in life.

Thank you, Dr. Coué, thank you from the bottom of my heart.

Dr. Robert Muller, Secretary of the Economic and Social Council of the United Nations, grew up in Alsace-Lorraine, son of a hatmaker. He fought in the French Resistance and was captured by the Nazis. He has served on diplomatic missions around the world. "Thank You, Dr. Coué" is an excerpt from Most of All, They Taught Me Happiness, *a lively, optimistic book of his experiences. Dr. Muller's "main purpose in writing my book was to reestablish a little more confidence in humanity and in our future." He is married to Margarita Gallo, a former UN diplomat from Chile.*

"Why had he been such a fool as to pry
into these people's business?

Tears for a Tailor

BY E.G. CHIPULINA

Humorous . . . an unusual way out of trouble.

TIME and progress had gradually lowered the status of Calle San Sebastian, once an elegant residential street in the city of Concepcion. Now it was grimy, and the asphalt surface was crumbling at the curbsides. Halfway down the street stood number 23, the roofless remnants of a once-proud house. A heavy, iron-grilled door led to a patio behind the façade, where a ragged assortment of makeshift dwellings leaned for support against the crumbling walls. The place smelt of onions, garlic, and cheap olive oil. And wandering around disconsolately, a few skinny hens pecked hopefully at the dirt between the remaining tiles.

Nearest the street entrance, Manolo the carpenter, who made a living supplying an undertaker with coffins at cut prices, planed away busily outside his workshop—a room barely twelve feet square which, at night-time, served as sleeping quarters for himself, his wife, and his twelve-year-old son. Against the rear wall the finished coffins were stacked and covered with an old canvas; not that he was ashamed of his work, but somehow it didn't seem right to leave them uncovered.

Outside a green door at the far end, a man stood warily peering in. In his hand he held a suitcase. The door led to a tiny kitchen, where a table occupied most of the space available. Beyond was a tailor's workshop.

The tailor was engaged in an argument with an intractable client. Jacinto Morales, the tailor, had a flat crooked nose which contrasted with the rest of his pointed features. He was slight and bony, and working long hours in poorly ventilated quarters had brought an unhealthy pallor to his cheeks. A battered pair of spectacles with thick lenses magnified his eyes to give him an expression of excitement out of all proportion to the triviality of the argument.

"But, señor Martinez," he implored, "how can I promise a thing I *know* I shall not be able to accomplish?"

"I have had my suits made here for ten years!"

Seated in a wide circle around the working table, three girls and a boy, all of them teenaged, sewed away impassively, occasionally casting a tired glance at the disputants. They had heard all this so many times before! Even at night, when they finally went to bed, the room seemed to echo with the demands of exacting clients.

"Surely . . ." persisted señor Martinez.

Jacinto caught sight of the man standing outside. His manner changed abruptly. "Not another word," he interrupted. "We are wasting time. For you, señor Martinez, I will accomplish the impossible. Call for your suit on Saturday." With these words he ushered out a bewildered but satisfied client.

"Please!" With a gesture, Jacinto invited the waiting man to enter, then clapped his hands. "Children!"

Almost automatically the four teenagers laid aside their work and trooped out of the room in single file. This was an everyday ritual. The more modest of their father's clients always insisted it was improper to try on new trousers in the children's presence.

"Well?" said Jacinto, as soon as they were alone. He pushed back his gray hairs nervously.

"From Gonzalo," said the man, handing him the suitcase. "He will send for it on Thursday, or perhaps Friday."

"I see," nodded Jacinto.

The man took out a wallet, selected a five hundred peseta note, and placed it on the table. Then, without another word, he left. Jacinto put the suitcase inside an old trunk which he locked carefully, and pocketed the money. How timely! The rent collector was due next morning.

It was about a year ago that one of Gonzalo's men had come, posing as a client, and discreetly asked him if he would like to earn a little extra money now and again. It had all sounded rather shady, but Jacinto had agreed. When one had four growing children to bring up on the modest income of a slum tailor one could not afford to be too particular. Of course, if Maria had been alive he would have thought twice. In time he had learnt many things: that a certain ring operated in Concepcion and elsewhere; that there was a mysterious Gonzalo behind it; that he himself was paid for the use of his workshop as a sort of transit center for smuggled or stolen goods—he wasn't quite sure which, and he was discreet enough not to ask.

Outside, Manolo the carpenter looked up as the shadow of the man, passing on his way to the street, darkened the gleaming plank of wood in front of him. The man was a stranger and his appearance rather incongruous with the surroundings. The irregular but frequent comings and goings of tough-looking men, invariably carrying suitcases or packages, were none of his business; but he couldn't help wondering. Instinctively, he knew they were up to no good. Still, "Each one to his own" and "Judge not" were worthy sayings. Manolo was a good Catholic; was not his son, Pepe, the best acolyte in the parish church of Santa Clara? Besides, Jacinto the tailor was his friend. So, without another thought, Manolo resumed his work.

Three weeks later, in the dead of night, Jacinto was awakened by a gentle rapping. For a moment he thought he had been dreaming, but the rapping continued. He rose, lit a candle, and went to the door.

"Who's there?" he whispered.

"From Gonzalo. Open quickly!" came the reply.

Jacinto opened the door, and three men staggered in. One of them was supported by the other two, and he seemed in the last stages of drunkenness. But there was blood; a little patch on his chest that glistened in the candlelight.

"What has happened?" Jacinto blinked. Without his spectacles he couldn't be sure.

"An accident," growled one of the men unpleasantly. "Quick now, put him under the table."

Laboriously, they slid him head first between the legs of the table, until his feet disappeared from view. The two men were sweating and panting heavily.

"I am going to get a car," said the smaller of the two. "He will stay here. In half an hour I will be back." He paused at the door. The sound of snoring could be heard from the room beyond. The man jerked his chin questioningly in the direction of the snoring.

"My children," explained Jacinto. "Don't worry. They sleep like logs."

This seemed to satisfy the man, and he disappeared into the darkness of the patio outside. Jacinto placed the candle on the table and put on his spectacles. The remaining man sat himself on the edge of the table and began to smoke. He puffed at the foul-smelling cigarette, staring at it, his face drawn and tense. Jacinto examined him surreptitiously. His youthful features were marred by a hardness, an indefinable permanent sneer pulling down the corners of his lips. In the poor light of the candle, his massive bulk was imposing.

A quarter of an hour passed, and the man had not as much as glanced up. And all the time he smoked incessantly, stamping out the stubs only half-smoked. Twenty minutes, and Jacinto began to feel uncomfortable. His imagination roamed, exploring the possibilities; trying to explain the silent form under the table, though in his heart he knew the answer. Half an hour, and the man glanced at his watch.

"Stay here! I am going outside to have a look."

The door closed noiselessly, and Jacinto was left with a—yes, he was sure of it now—corpse under his kitchen table. He looked down, horrified, but it was too dark to see. A curiosity stronger than horror moved him to pick up the candle. Holding it with a shaking hand, he knelt on the floor. The still figure wore an old trenchcoat, which seemed far too large. He examined the stain. There was no doubt that it was blood, but he saw no wound. Very carefully, he undid the buttons, and started violently at what he saw. It was not the glaring wound that shocked him, but the gray-green cloth the knife had rent—the uniform of a customs officer.

Without warning, the door opened and the two men walked in. They waited while Jacinto crawled with difficulty from under the table. For a second they stared at him through narrowed eyes, but they said nothing. Quickly they bent down and dragged the body from under the table. Each of them put his neck under one of the dead man's armpits, and together they hoisted him up. They staggered out to the patio. The small man turned his head and smiled—a smile in which his eyes took no part—his gold teeth glinting in the candlelight.

"Gonzalo will pay you extra money for this service," he whispered.

Jacinto watched the darkness swallow them up. He heard the sound of a car engine starting, then with a whine it was gone. He closed the door and leaned against it. Extra money! What did they take him for? An idiot? A child? He had worked long enough with them to know their ways. He was as good as dead. He had seen more than was good for him, and Gonzalo wouldn't fancy having a witness at large. Tomorrow they would come. A ride in the car, far out into the country; a desolate spot, a shot in the nape of the neck. Holy Mary! Why had he been such a fool as to pry into these people's business? Trembling, Jacinto crept between the sheets, on a mattress spread on a floor littered with bits of cloth, thread, and fragments of paper patterns.

The warmth of the bed dispelled his gloomy mood, and brought back hope. Surely there was a way out! But not the obvious way. Running away to another town would solve nothing. They would eventually track him down, and anyway, he had no money for train fare. What about his good friend Manolo the carpenter? But Manolo had a wife and son to support, and two elderly aunts who lived next door. No! It wasn't right to ask him for a loan—even if he did have the money. But perhaps Manolo could help in another way, if he confided in him. Manolo was clever. He didn't say very much, but the little he said was sensible.

Jacinto didn't sleep the rest of the night. He felt like a prisoner in the death-cell. At the first signs of daylight, he rose and went to visit his friend, the carpenter, who started work with the dawn.

In the early hours of the following morning, the dimly lit Calle San Sebastian was deserted. An old Citroen rumbled up and stopped opposite number 23. Two men emerged, looked about them, and walked in past the iron gates. Once inside the dark patio, one of them produced a torch and began to illuminate the doors briefly, one by one, until he found what he wanted—a green door. Without knocking, they entered. Inside there was a peculiar smell of flowers, reminiscent of the inside of a church, but blended with a stronger one of onions and other less definable cooking smells.

As they passed into the inner room, their eyebrows rose slightly; their grim, tense faces relaxed almost imperceptibly, and a smile hovered momentarily on their lips.

They looked at each other and shrugged in unison. The tailor's working table was placed in the center of the room. On it was an open coffin with gleaming brass handles, its varnished surface reflecting the flickering light of the candles which stood at the four corners of the table. Around the coffin were bunches of flowers. A priest stood at the foot of the coffin, open missal in hand, intoning prayers in a mournful sing-song voice. At his elbow, a young acolyte responded at the appropriate pauses, his subdued falsetto contrasting with the deep bass of the priest. In the background four youngsters, three girls and a boy, their eyes irritated with weeping, sat huddled together on a folding canvas bed. Two elderly ladies, their eyes turned ceilingwards, fumbled with strings of beads, and moved their lips silently. Near the door, a fat, middle-aged woman sat on a wicker chair, her hands clasped piously against her ample bosom.

The two men stepped forward to get a better view of the dead man. There was no doubt he was the tailor. "A broken nose—like a boxer," they had been told. He was pale, even for a corpse. "Big eyes," Gonzalo had said. But in death they seemed to have shrunk. His cheeks had sunk into his face, and his bony hands had been folded on his chest.

Without a word the men turned on their heels and made for the door. Here one of them paused to look back. For a moment his hard, cold eyes softened. The tailor's death had saved him from an unpleasant and risky job. He felt indebted to the deceased. Impulsively he pulled out a handful of banknotes and flung them carelessly on the kitchen table. Then he was gone.

For some minutes the scene in the room remained unchanged. Suddenly the priest paused in his chanting, and motioned to the tailor's son with his head. The boy rose and went out. After a while he returned.

"They have gone," he said, wiping his eyes. "Phew! How those onions sting!"

Slowly the corpse came back to life, sat up and stretched his cramped limbs. From a pocket he produced his false teeth and replaced them; from another, his spectacles. He regarded the priest, gratitude in his eyes.

"Manolo, you are a genius," he said.

Manolo brushed aside the compliment, and turned to the acolyte. "Here, son," he said, removing his richly embroidered robes. "You'd better take these back before Padre Esteban starts looking for them. The first Mass at Santa Clara is at six."

Manolo's elderly aunts put their beads down and thanked God. The tailor's son was counting the notes on the kitchen table.

"Papa!" he called excitedly. "There's more than a thousand pesetas here."

"What?" Jacinto climbed out of the coffin. "What's that?"

"The money the man left."

"A thousand pesetas!" whispered Jacinto. "Quick, boy, go over to the railway offices and get us five tickets on the early train to Barcelona."

E.G. Chipulina's "The Man on the Gray Horse" appeared in SSI No. 13, "Presumed Dead" in SSI No. 18. Mr. Chipulina's short stories and other pieces are published in Scotland, England and the USA. After more than 15 years of part-time writing, he "recently chucked a good job to launch out into full-time writing." His love for language and literature is closely matched by a love for painting and sketching. Mr. Chipulina credits his cheerful wife with encouraging his writing career.

"Unfortunately for them I got wind of the plot while it was being hatched.

Don Chepe

BY VICTOR PERERA

Akin to King Canute, a baronial Guatemalan coffee planter tries to hold back the tide.

I had returned to Guatemala City for a brief stay, fresh from two years of teaching in a New York women's college and a year in Europe, when I learned that a former schoolmate, Gustavo Lopez, was our next-door neighbor. He dropped in for coffee that very evening and invited me to accompany him the next day on his monthly tour of coffee plantations. Gustavo was a travelling agent for a U.S. plastics concern, and it was his job to create a demand, among planters, for the company's polyethylene gadgets. I remembered Gustavo as an easy-going cheerful sort who got along well with our martinet Jesuit teachers. We had shared a bond of a kind in that he had been the only *mestizo* (Spanish father, Indian mother) in a class of pedigreed white Catholics, and I the only foreigner. Gustavo had a mustache now, and his curly black hair was slicked down with pomade. His boyish dimples had vanished behind the taut edges of a lantern jaw. He said he planned to interview one or two planters on the Pacific Coast and pay a social call on an old family acquaintance, a Sevillian planter named José—Chepe—Ramírez. Don Chepe, Gustavo assured me, was an exceptional fellow, a lineal descendant of Hernán Cortes and one of the very few pro-Franco Spanish exiles settled in Guatemala.

"Don Chepe is the last of his kind," Gustavo said. "He is the last true Spaniard in Guatemala, and the interesting thing is he's finally becoming aware of it."

I accepted Gustavo's invitation at once, not only for the chance to meet this latter-day conquistador, but because it would give me my first look at a coffee finca. Although I had grown up in Guatemala and returned several times on summer holiday, I had never set foot in one of these feudal outposts—the notorious strongholds of political reaction in Central America.

It was still dark when we left the city in Gustavo's Volkswagen. The gray humped profile of Pacaya Volcano rose directly ahead, a curl of smoke rising from its cone. After an hour we passed the little Indian town of Palin and began the rapid descent into the plains. We dropped twenty-five hundred feet in three or four miles of spiralling road, my ears popping continuously as the rolling hills of the highland gave way to the lush flatland of the *tierra caliente*. As my senses adjusted to the heat, the sounds of the lowland resolved into a high-frequency hum. The air grew thick with insects and winged creatures, some of which crashed with a *splat* on our windshield. Lizards of all sizes zipped across the road; black striated patches remained where an unwary iguana had been ground into the asphalt.

We stopped for a bite to eat in Escuintla, a fly-blown trading town midway to the sea. On our way out Gustavo stopped to send a telegram to Estelita, his fiancée in Guatemala City. This was a daily ritual whenever he went on the road, and it taxed all his ingenuity to crowd as much poetic sentiment as possible into a dozen pithy words. For inspiration he carried several books in the glove compartment, among them a Spanish edition of the Bible, the sonnets of Shakespeare and Petrarch, the Rubaiyat and—at the bottom of the heap—a selection from Casanova's letters. That morning he sent her a line from the Song of Songs in which he likened Estelita's hair to a flock of goats in Gilead. "It's only nine words long," he said, grinning happily. "I had enough left for 'a million kisses.' "

"But won't she recognize the source?"

"Estelita? She only reads the New Testament . . . She is from a very Catholic family."

We turned westward and followed a parallel course with the Pacific piedmont for the remainder of the afternoon. Just before nightfall we arrived in Malacatán, a few miles from the Mexican border. Gustavo parked the car in the plaza and we checked in at the traveler's hotel across the street. Malacatán is a very hot, somnolent town of about a thousand white and *mestizo* residents, collectively called *ladinos*. On the afternoon of our visit the oppressive heat was charged with rumors of an imminent guerilla raid from the mountains of San Marcos. On an earlier raid a week before the Castroist rebels had kidnaped the mayor of the town and three of its wealthiest tradesmen, and held them for ransom. The ransom was paid, but only the mayor had been returned. The three *ladinos* were executed by the guerrillas as enemies of the Revolution.

I went out for a stroll after dinner, half-hoping to catch the guerrillas in action. But even they couldn't shake Malacatán from its torpor. Two hours after sunset it resembled a ghost town. Not a soul walked the streets, not a leaf stirred in the trees of the park. The airless night pressed down on the rooftops like a lid, and snuffed out even the sense of menace. I walked twice around the plaza, trying to fix in my mind an awareness of change, of inner growth, of a return to familiar surroundings after a long absence. But nothing in the sleepy aspect of this little town revealed the violence of Guatemalan politics, or—as I had begun to realize at dinner the night before—the brutalizing effect of that violence on my family and friends. The moon cast an eerie pallor on the limestone façade of the church and on the town hall next to it. From the center of the square the branches of a giant ceiba reached out to the farthest roof, enfolding the town in a smothering embrace.

We rose at dawn the next morning, ate a sturdy breakfast of

black beans, tortillas and fried eggs "rancher style" and headed south toward the sea, to visit our first finca. By evening we would end up at Don Chepe's plantation. The weather was perfect. The miasma of the lowland had not yet risen from the forest and a crayon-yellow sun hung just above the treetops. We stopped in town to buy some fruits, and to dispatch that morning's telegram to Estelita. Gustavo had slept poorly the night before and was in a surly temper. After a grim search in his anthologies he found a verse from Calderón's *Life is a Dream* that reflected his mood: "What is Life? An illusion, a shadow, a fiction . . ." He tacked on the usual "a million kisses," and stepped out of the telegraph office with a jaunty air, restored to himself.

An hour later we heard over the car radio that four masked men had broken into a finca near Malacatán the night before and machine-gunned to death the owner and his *administrador*.

"F.A.R. guerrillas," Gustavo said drily. "They've started again." We drove the rest of the way in silence.

The finca we visited belonged to a young German planter named Schulte. To get to it we drove off the tarred road and travelled uphill for several miles on a rutted jeep track. At last we passed a stone gate, and the anarchy of tropical vegetation gave way to a Euclidean landscape of coffee trees. The glossy green bushes, all groomed to an even six feet, spread out on either side of a gentle slope. The harvest season had started and the branches dipped low with crimson berries.

Schulte intercepted us at the gate with a cordial smile, but did not ask us inside his house. He looked about twenty-five, was blond and blue-eyed, an inch or two taller than his coffee trees. Gustavo's manner with him was terse and businesslike but with a hint of servility to ease the transaction along, like a smoothing drop of lubricant. Schulte, I learned, had been the first of Gustavo's clients to purchase the plastic implements in sizable quantities. After a brisk conference at the gate he placed an order for two thousand polyethylene germinator sacks and a hundred meters of fumigation hose and then escorted us to the car, still smiling cordially but formal, remote, as if to impress on us he had no time for the customary amenities.

The sun grew hotter as we pushed nearer the coast, and the enervating humidity closed around us like a blanket. We ate some oranges we had bought in Malacatán, scratched almost sensuously at the wounds inflicted on our bodies by mosquitoes, gnats, flies, leeches. I had balked at buying sweets in the town market because they were incrusted with honeybees. Gustavo scorned my squeamishness, flipped a sweet into his mouth without bothering to inspect it. "What doesn't kill, fattens," he said, citing the proverb that is an axiom of survival in the lowland.

After we'd eaten I pressed Gustavo for more background on Don Chepe, whom I began to envision as something of an *enfant terrible* among coffee planters.

"You will like him," he said. "He is very animated. He used to be a professional soccer-player in Spain until he damaged his legs in a car accident. Then a German planter—Schulte's father, in fact—met him in Madrid and invited him to come to Guatemala to administer his fincas. After Schulte died in Argentina Don Chepe bought a finca of his own."

"What are his politics?"

"Reactionary, of course, like all planters. He had been a Falangist in Spain. Had he remained there for the Civil War, he would probably have been an officer in Franco's army."

I asked if Don Chepe had been hurt at all by Arbenz's Agrarian Reform in the early Fifties, and Gustavo said he had, but not as much as United Fruit and other large foreign-owned holdings. He said none of his property was confiscated and parcelled out to the peasants because nearly all of it had been cultivated, and the Reform laws applied only to untilled land.

"Then how was he affected?"

"Insurrection. Labor agitators infiltrated the finca during the harvest and goaded the *mozos* into demanding more pay."

"And he gave in?"

"Don Chepe?" Gustavo snorted. "It's clear you don't know him. That man is a tiger." He tapped his elbow suggestively. "And also very tight. After all, he's Andaluz."

I became impatient. "Well then, what happened?"

This was a mistake. He smiled at me in a slow, taunting manner he had, and tossed me another proverb: "Patience, bedbug, the night is long."

"All right," I said. "So he shot them."

"Guess again."

"He tore out their bowels and fed them to his pigs."

He laughed. "You've been seeing too many cowboy pictures. He simply gathered a dozen of his loyal men and chased the troublemakers out of the finca."

I sat back. "That's *all?*"

"There was one hitch. The leader of the rebels was Don Chepe's foreman, who also happens to be his brother-in-law. It was a hard blow to his pride. Don Chepe, you see, belongs to the old school of gentlemen planters who expect absolute loyalty from their workers in exchange for three meals and a roof over their heads. Like most Spaniards he is a medievalist at heart, a feudal baron . . . And he is also pig-headed, like my father."

I asked how the foreman had come to be Don Chepe's brother-in-law and he said that after buying his own finca Don Chepe had married an Indian woman. Doña Tomasina, the daughter of a local village *cacique* or chieftain. "She was his housekeeper and concubine for several years, and he married her only after she bore him a daughter. The foreman was Doña Tomasina's younger brother."

"It all sounds very incestuous," I said. My curiosity was now fully aroused, but Gustavo was bent on enlarging on Don Chepe's pigheadedness, particularly in regard to plastics.

"Don Chepe thinks plastics are the invention of the Devil. He says they rob coffee-planting of its dignity." His voice hoarsened with irritation. "He won't touch synthetics of any kind. Nearly all the processing on his plant is done by hand—"

"How does he keep up with the competition?"

"Who can say?" He drove one-handed, using the other to shape an explanation. "His coffee is good quality, there is no denying that—the best you can find in the region. And he experiments, he experiments all the time with different fertilizers, with new shading and pruning methods. He has a small orchard set apart from the main *cafetal* where he likes to tinker with the soil, and plants in it every variety of African and Arabic coffee, including some hybrids of his own. He's a dreamer. He's always looking for the ideal blend . . . But he knows coffee. There is no denying that."

"I find that rather admirable," I said, having lived half my life under the lengthening shadow of automation.

Gustavo pounded his fist on the dashboard. "But he does not produce enough! Today, the demand is for quantity, not quality." He swept his arm over the green expanse of banana trees outside the car window. "Look at United Fruit! Do you think it makes any difference to the Yankee consumer what kind of tree his bananas come from? For all he knows, or cares, they could grow under the ground, like potatoes. Do you think the buyer cares what infinitesimal fraction of his morning cup of coffee is the best quality Arabica grown on the Pacific coast of Guatemala by a certain Don Chepe Ramirez? The Yankee importers want quantity. Mass production. They're interested in the maximum bags of raw coffee that can be extracted from a single tree. That's how it is with United Fruit. If one of their plantations isn't producing enough bananas, they send down an efficiency expert from New York."

"Then how does Don Chepe survive?"

Gustavo threw up his hands and steered with his knees, a favorite ploy of his. "Because among the middlemen who buy coffee for the big companies there are still left a few sentimentalists like Don Chepe, and they pay him the highest prices on the market . . . But don't worry, economics will weed them out."

"Probably," I said.

"Supply and demand, supply and demand," chanted Gustavo, clicking his teeth. "That is all that matters in this world."

I kept at Gustavo for more information during the remainder of the afternoon, scattering my queries so as not to appear over-eager, and learned that Teresita, Don Chepe's daughter, was a slender, green-eyed beauty of seventeen, and a great favorite of her father.

"You'll meet her," he said, with a lubricious wink. "She's ripened nicely, very nicely. The last time I visited the finca she and Don Chepe had a quarrel about the rebel guerrilla activities. They have a strong affection for one another but she fought him tooth and nail, like a wild animal." He shook his head. "I am afraid Teresita may turn communist, like her uncle Ramiro, and that is a shame because she is a real beauty. If I wasn't already promised to my Estelita—*por Dios!*—I would try a pass at her myself, and to hell with her politics!"

We drove two hours more in the hot sun, our throats parched and coated with dust, until we came to an intersection where the rugged coastal road meets the hardtop from the city. About three miles beyond, on the southern tip of a raised plateau that overlooked the sea, we could make out the ant-like structures of Don Chepe's finca, perched two thousand feet above the plains. Gustavo's car labored up the winding slope in first gear. As we neared the top a green patch of coffee trees appeared on our left, vanished behind a granite wall, reappeared and vanished again on each twist of the road. Clouds of dust lifted behind us, through which we had tonic glimpses of the smooth blue Pacific. Near the summit we came to a large frame house, the finca's *casa grande*. I was struck by the rundown state of Don Chepe's residence. There were unsightly gaps in the tiled roof and the pock-marked greenish façade was badly in need of a coat of paint. A flock of *zopilotes*, the ubiquitous black vultures of the tropics, sunned unmolested on the drain-pipe. They looked, with their slack coats and beaked purposeful stares, like a gathering of morticians.

Gustavo waved to a solitary figure on the veranda, and Don Chepe came down the steps to greet us. He was a small, wiry man of about fifty, with the lightly toasted complexion of the Andaluz. A beret eclipsed one side of his head. I was surprised to see that he limped rather heavily and needed a cane for support. Any suggestion of frailty, however, was banished by his quick smile and firm handshake.

"*Bienvenido amigo López,*" he said, grasping Gustovao's shoulder in a strong *abrazo*. "I began to fear we wouldn't see you this time around."

"I've been a little delayed." Gustavo introduced me as his excuse.

"It is a great pleasure," Don Chepe said, squeezing my hand as though he meant it. "Come inside. Come inside." He ushered us to a corner of the veranda, sat us around a brown wicker table. On the wall opposite hung a faded tapestry of the Guirnalda, Sevilla's splendid Moorish tower. Our view of the courtyard was screened by a spray of scarlet bougainvillaea that scaled the porch columns to the roof. Huge pots of dripping ferns hung from the eaves, one to each column. A pet macaw, large as a rooster, with iridescent blue and red feathers, waddled to and fro on the veranda rail, squawking aloud and calling "Mariamariamariamariamaria."

"And how is your esteemed father?" Don Chepe asked Gustavo. "These eyes have not lit on his shining person in several months. Is he ailing?"

"In a manner of speaking," Gustavo smiled. "He is growing blisters in the seat of his pants."

"I see, I see." Don Chepe laughed. "Our Don Manuel is beginning to value his comforts. Has he been sucking the—" He mimed the bottle with his thumb.

"No more than usual. And his half-dozen cigars a day. The doctors tell him he has high blood-pressure, but I think he has just lost ambition."

"*Bien*, I understand. Old age is setting in. Well, let it be, he has earned his little rest. And so the burdens of the family have fallen on your shoulders, is that it?"

Gustavo shrugged stoically. "What can be done? One hasn't much choice in this life."

"Of course. Quite so." He rubbed his chin with the grip of his cane. "Tell me, what are you selling these days, anything new?"

"Nothing you could use, Don Chepe. Plastics, as usual. My company has brought out a germinator sack that is proving quite a success."

"A germinator sack . . . made of plastic? You're pulling my leg."

"It's true, Don Chepe. What is more, it is selling very well. It has proven to be economical. Don Enrique Schulte has been using it this season and has already reduced his labor costs by twenty-five percent."

"Young Schulte is a very intelligent planter," Don Chepe said slowly. "He is more intelligent than his father was. But I'm not convinced he's a better man." He turned to me and asked if I had met the younger Schulte on our visit to his finca. I said I had seen him briefly and he seemed a forthright, practical-minded man.

"Very practical," Don Chepe agreed. "And very intelligent. Don Federico would be proud to see how well he is managing the finca. But he lacks his father's warmth, the spark of humanity. Poor Don Federico. He died in Buenos Aires, you know, twelve years ago. President Ubico exiled him in '43 and he lived the rest of his years a lonely, embittered man. Young Schulte is a new breed of German planter, a post war breed that I can respect and even admire but don't particularly like. Since Don Federico's passing I have not set foot in that finca."

"—And not only Schulte," cut in Gustavo, not to be put off. "More than half the planters in the region will start using these sacks next year. To be perfectly frank, Don Chepe, I think the competition will get tough on you in the coming seasons."

"I'm not troubled by the competition," Don Chepe said. "I'm not operating a finca to set production records." He smiled. "We'll walk down to the orchard in a little while. Remember those Robusta coffee seeds I had sent from Ethiopia? I've been crossing them with some of my high-grade Arabica, and I think I may have an interesting new strain on my hands . . . a most interesting strain."

"I would be delighted to see it," Gustavo said, formal.

"Good. But you must be parched after the long drive in the sun. Let us have a little something to lift our spirits . . . Maria!" He called down the long dark corridor that led to the servants' quarters. Within seconds an Indian domestic appeared. She wore a plain peasant blouse and a long blue skirt, and covered her mouth with one hand as if to conceal laughter.

"You called, Don Chepe?" She dropped her hand and I saw she was in her late teens, and comely.

"Yes, Maria, fetch me the flask with the *manzanilla* from the cellar, and tell Doña Tomasina and Teresita to come down. We have guests."

"Right away, Don Chepe." Still smiling, she spun around on bare heels and sailed down the corridor, switching her long skirt.

The macaw followed her along the rail, squawking and calling her name, but she paid it no heed.

Don Chepe then asked where I was from and what I did. I told him I was a teacher, and had been abroad for a number of years. In passing I mentioned I had been fortunate to visit Sevilla during the fair the previous April.

"*Hombre!*" His face lit up. "Why didn't you say so in the first place? How did you like it? How long were you there? What bullfights did you see?" Before I could reply he launched into a passionate reminiscence, enlivened with broad gestures, of his youthful experiences at the fair. He described the gaiety and color, the dancing in the streets, the beautiful women and the famous matadors he had known. His accent changed as he spoke; he began swallowing consonants and a flamenco inflection stole into his voice.

"I went back for the *feria* in '67," he said, turning sober. "It was no longer the same. The gaiety, the *alegría* was still there, and the Sevillanas in their crinoline skirts were as handsome as ever. But the tourists, my God, the tourists were everywhere . . . like locusts. They did not dance, they did not drink, they only walked from one end of the fairground to the other, sniffing the wines in the booths, pinching the fruits, ogling our women, and snapping their machines—click here, click there—like scavengers." He slapped the table. "They turned Sevilla into a bazaar . . . Don't you agree?"

"More or less," I temporized, having been a tourist there myself.

"But tell me, were you in Sevilla for the Holy Week?"

I said I had hoped to be, but hadn't found lodging and so spent it in Málaga instead.

"Málaga? Come now, Málaga is a pretty town, it has a quaint view of the sea, but it is no place to pass the Holy Week." He shook his head, fixed me with a look of reproach. "Did you see the processions?"

"Only the first one. I found it disappointing."

"Of course! Of course it was disappointing. In Málaga there is no longer a tradition—it was broken by the war. They began the *pasos* again ten years ago to attract tourists."

I said I had heard something to that effect from a medical student in my pension, before his lips were buttoned by the other residents.

"Naturally. And with good reason. But it is no secret, I assure you, it is an established fact. In Sevilla the Holy Week celebrations are serious. They are a part of an authentic tradition that dates back many centuries. They are—how shall I say it—an expression of sincere religious emotion . . . I'll tell you a little story." He leaned forward, his face tensed with feeling . . . "When I was thirteen my father, a stonemason in the cathedral, drove a chisel through his hand to prove himself worthy of carrying Our Lady of Sorrows in the procession that year. The hand became badly infected, and when Good Friday came there was no one to take his place. With the backing of younger members of our Brotherhood I persuaded my father to let me substitute for him. Although barely thirteen, you see, I had already attained my present size, and I was brash.

"Early the next morning we started out from the Church of San Lorenzo. I felt strong and fresh, and eager to prove to my *Virgencita*—and to my father, naturally—that I was worthy of my charge. But after two hours of bearing her through the Calle de las Sierpes I was ready to collapse from weariness and the ache in all my bones. Do you know what it is to carry a Holy Image through those streets in the heat of a Sevillian April, step by agonizing step, swaying in rhythm to drum and trumpets, and the multitudes pressing around you to fling garlands, cheering, shouting, pleading that you hold her head higher, that you execute the steps more slowly, that you sway more to this side or the other . . ." He paused to light a cigar he had been rolling in his fingers. "We noticed after a time that the bearers ahead of us were resting their image more and more frequently, and were no longer swaying to the drum beat. The temptation to imitate them was very strong. But every time we felt our energies about to give out, and our legs ready to fold under the weight, someone would leap out of the crowds or lean over a balcony and deliver a *saeta*: a spontaneous arrow of song wrenched from the roots of the soul, in praise and adoration of Our Blessed Lady. It might be anyone—a gypsy rag-picker, a merchant, or a first-class tenor—it hardly mattered so long as the feeling was true." His eyes widened. "And it would be a deliverance . . . an inspiration. The weariness and the pains melted away, and we carried our Virgin erect, proud, taller and more beautiful than all the others. At first it had only been pride, you see, personal pride and loyalty to Our Lady that sustained us. It had been almost a competition. But after someone delivered a beautiful *saeta* it became more than just pride, or a test of endurance. Much more. It was emotion, a pure religious emotion." He wiped his eyes. "*That* is Holy Week in Sevilla. In Málaga, you know what they do? They pay dockworkers so many *pesetas* to carry the images and hire an opera singer to deliver the *saetas*. *That* is Holy Week in Málaga!"

Maria had come in in the middle of Don Chepe's reminiscence and watched him with her head bent to one side, like a child. When he noticed her next to him, Don Chepe snatched the wineskin from her hands. "About time, wench!" he roared, and sent her sprawling with a resounding whack on the rump.

"Doña Tomasina says she will be down right away," Maria said from the floor, with unruffled aplomb.

"And Teresita?"

She lifted one shoulder. "I knocked on her door and there was no answer."

"Off with you then, and tell them not to hurry. We are provided for." Maria skimmed down the corridor with the impudent switch of her skirts and a saucy smile on her face.

"And now, to gladden our kidneys, as they say in my region." Don Chepe raised the goatskin *bota* up high and delivered a long gypsy eulogy to the sweetness of Sevillian wines, the gaiety of her dances, the unsurpassed loveliness of her women. To confound the sacred and the profane altogether beyond distinguishing he capped this with a toast to "the most beautiful virgin in all Spain—Our Lady of Sorrows."

"Olé!" called Gustavo, rising to the occasion.

We passed the wineskin around several times as Don Chepe, growing more garrulous with each round, sketched for us a beguiling portrait of Teresita riding through the fairground on a white stallion, garbed as an *amazona* in black Cordoba hat, toreador jacket and pants, a flaming camellia behind her ear.

"Ay my soul what a sight. She was not yet fourteen, but the gallants trailed behind her like bloodhounds on the scent. I had to keep one eye peeled —like this—or they would have absconded with her, horse and all."

"It's a pity I could not be there to be counted with her admirers," Gustavo said.

Don Chepe laughed, tickled by the compliment. "I know you like I know the lines of my hand, you rogue. A little bird has told me of your escapades in the city." He poked Gustavo's leg with his cane. "But what is this I hear of your becoming serious with a young girl of society?"

Gustavo flushed, lowered his eyes. "It was a moment of weakness . . . I must be growing old."

"Oh so it's *that* serious, eh? Well, and why not? You're a man of the world now, responsible and self-supporting, a prince among traveling agents and future Caesar of the plastics industry . . ." He drank a toast to this, eyes sparkling merrily. "Tell me, what is the name of this anointed creature?"

"Estela Quevedo."

"Quevedo, eh?" He stroked his chin. "Not the Quevedos of the cement factories?"

"The same."

"A well-connected family. I see you're not wasting yourself on the first breath of spring to tickle your nostrils." Gustavo stared at the floor as Don Chepe rubbed his chin thoughtfully. "Quevedo . . . I knew a cousin of theirs in Madrid. A marquis. Have I told you that story? He was something of a dandy, a member of the idle rich. But tell me, I'm curious, have you met with any . . . unpleasantness from the family?"

Gustavo cleared his throat. "A little, yes. But only from the father. Doña Inez has been very kind to me."

"Yes yes, I see. Well, don't brood over it. A little reticence is to be expected from these blue-blooded families. They tend to forget they're no longer in Spain." He raised the wineskin and quaffed the last of its contents. "They'll come around in due time."

We were set to leave on our tour of the finca when a stocky woman walked in. She was dressed in a native blouse and skirt and incongruous brown pumps. Her complexion was a shade lighter than Maria's, although they both had the high Mongoloid cheekbones of descendants of the Maya.

"Ah there you are," Don Chepe said. "What's taken you so long? Where is Teresita?"

"I've been washing her hair, Don Chepe. She'll be down a little later."

"Washing her hair? At this ungodly hour? Well, never mind. Just tell Maria to bring us another flask of manzanilla from the cellar. I'm taking my guests to see the orchard."

"Very well, Don Chepe." She stood her ground. "Shall I tell Maria to set two more places for dinner?"

"Of course, woman. Of course they're staying for dinner." Gustavo protested that we had a long drive before us and had best not impose, but Don Chepe was adamant. Doña Tomasina listened patiently until it became evident that Gustavo would give in first; then she turned and slipped noiselessly away, without waiting to be introduced.

Don Chepe's orchard was on the western slope of the plateau, facing the ocean. To reach it we cut across a corner of the plantation where a troop of pickers, led by a "corporal" with a signal trumpet, were systematically stripping the trees of ripe berries. From an airplane they would look like a busy army of leaf-cutting ants.

We emerged from the *cafetal* and walked along the bamboo stile that marked off the laborers' compound. On our left stood a neat row of tiled cottages occupied by the resident *mozos*. The seasonal pickers' quarters, a rabbit warren of thatched huts, began fifty yards beyond, where the slope of the plateau grew steeper. Attached to each of these huts was a small apron of clayey soil for raising corn and beans: the proverbial *milpa* of the Indian farmer.

"The Indian loves disorder," Don Chepe said. "That is why I let him build his home to suit his tastes. As you can see, they have left the best tract of land unoccupied and have crowded their huts in one corner."

"They are like sheep," Gustavo said, and Don Chepe nodded agreement.

"It is true. The Indian is very sociable. If you present him with large parcels of fertile land, as Arbenz's government was doing in the early Fifties, he will plant a small *milpa* in one corner and allow the rest to go to seed. That is why agrarian reform will never succeed in this country. Leave the Indian on his own and he will grow beans and corn for his tortillas, raise a few chickens, and maybe, if he is very ambitious, he will keep two or three head of cattle. Whatever else he needs he can barter some chickens for at the market. If you give him more than that, he doesn't know what to do with it; he becomes confused, and ends by resenting you. Give him a tractor and try to teach him crop rotation and he will only get distracted, he will lose interest, and the tractor will be left to rust in the fields."

"Quite right," concurred Gustavo, as Don Chepe stopped on his tracks to drive home his point.

"The Indian is designed by nature so he can function best on a diet of bare subsistence: corn and beans. That is all he needs. If you try to enrich his diet, he will get indigestion and ulcers. *Indigestion and ulcers,*" he repeated, as if airing a pet theory he had long ago committed to memory.

"Or even worse," injected Gustavo, "he will grow fat. And a fat Indian is a dead Indian because he could never walk the thirty or forty kilometers to sell his produce."

We approached a small hut that stood some distance from the rest. Its roof of palm thatch was tilted at a precarious angle and its bamboo supports were all askew, like the bars of a marimba. Thick blue smoke poured from the walls, scattering ash and cinders in all directions. As we came closer I caught the pungent, unmistakable odor of toasting maize. I peeped between the slats at a kneeling woman fanning an open fire, a stack of tortillas by her side. Two naked infants sprawled on the earth floor, their bellies swollen from hookworm, while a third rolled in the dust with a squealing pig.

At the far end of the workers' compound, or *rancheria*, Don Chepe stopped to point out a discarded roll of rusted barbed wire.

"In the time of Arbenz I had to put up a stockade to keep out government spies. They would come down disguised as pickers and hire themselves out so they could spread their Bolshevik filth from within." He smiled, tapped his temple. "But I always outwitted them—you know how?" He asked me to hold out my hands, and rubbed the palms with the tip of his cane. "Their hands. You can always tell an experienced coffee picker by his hands."

"Then you had no trouble with your men?" I asked, emboldened by the wine and by his seeming high spirits.

The flush of animation fled from Don Chepe's face and then rekindled, like a candle in a gust of wind. "Yes," he said, "unfortunately I did. I lost four of my men. It's an interesting story . . ." He stopped to take a swig of *manzanilla* and hobbled on, smiting at weeds with his cane. "One of these men, their leader, is my wife's brother Ramiro, who had been my foreman for fifteen years. One Sunday night he met a government agent a local *cantina* and this man poisoned Ramiro's mind against me. He told him—well, you can imagine—that the finca belonged to the workers as much as the landlord; that the portions of land not under cultivation were legally theirs—and all the rest of the claptrap. They met in secret several times and finally the Bolshevik persuaded him to collect a few habitual malcontents and to approach me with a demand for more pay. If I didn't agree to their terms, they would threaten to strike. Their plan, you see, was to win the first test and then bleed from me bigger and bigger concessions until I was forced to hand over half the plantation." He spat on the ground. "The ungrateful wretches . . . Unfortunately for them I got wind of the plot while it was being hatched. Late that night I loaded my carbine, gathered a dozen men whose loyalty I could count on, and called on Ramiro and his three cohorts in their quarters. I ordered them to leave the finca inside of two hours, and to warn the Bolshevik that I would shoot him on sight if I caught him meddling again with my men." He chuckled softly at the memory of the laborers' ashen faces when he charged in on them in the dead of night. "Naturally I had no choice. I had to act at once and show no vacillation . . . But one question pursues me to this day. I ask myself if they really had the *cojones* to carry out the plot. I muse on that frequently . . ."

"And do you know what became of them?" I asked.

"Yes. They joined a peasant labor movement in the Capital. After the defeat of Arbenz by Castillo Armas in 1954 the leaders of the movement fled to San Salvador, and Ramiro and his cronies were thrown in jail. Four years ago many political prisoners were granted amnesty, among them Ramiro. I've heard that he's been in Mexico receiving guerrilla training, and there are rumors that he recently came back across the border and joined the Communist rebels in the mountains of San Marcos. But these are only rumors. The only certainty is that he is out of jail."

We had reached the crest of the plateau and beheld the Pacific at our feet, spread flat against the horizon like a blue tiled floor. Don Chepe's orchard was to our right, on a gentle decline that gave it ideal exposure to sunlight and wind. It was late afternoon and the slanting rays dyed the crowns of the coffee trees a soft yellow. The precise orderliness of the orchard contrasted sharply with the careless jumble of the seasonal pickers' compound; although it covered nearly as large an area, all the underbrush had been cleared and the hedgerows that defined its borders were painstakingly trimmed. The effect was one of exquisite care and geometrical exactness, as in a Moorish garden.

Don Chepe led us to a small nursery at the far end of the orchard. Ten rows of coffee saplings, each swaddled in its separate diaper of green banana leaf, lay under a flat canopy of palm thatch.

"This is my new hybrid," Don Chepe said, kneeling by a row of tender shoots—hardly a week old—that were entering what he called the "*soldadito*" stage: tiny soldiers with coiled green hats on parade. He scooped up a handful of thick black soil and sifted it slowly, fingering its texture. "As you can see I have planted them in fresh volcanic soil."

Gustavo said, "I understand there's been some activity near here recently."

Don Chepe nodded. "A few tremors, nothing major—at least not yet. This ash is from a recent eruption around Coatepeque, twenty kilometers north of here. There a new volcano is coming up. I went to a good deal of trouble, I needn't tell you, to collect a few truckloads of this. But it was well worth it. Volcanic ash makes the richest natural fertilizer cover in the world." He stood up, smiling, as black soil streamed from his hands. "There is nothing I won't do for my coffee. Nothing—" he grinned at Gustavo— "except perhaps plastics. There I draw the line."

On our return we took a shortcut through the *rancheria* and were detained midway by a thin reedy voice that sang to the scraping of a guitar. A group of *mozos*, their work done for the day, had gathered around the water well to idle away an hour. The singing ceased abruptly at our approach, but not before we verified that it had issued from a very small boy—hardly eight or nine—who wore his straw hat down to the bridge of his nose. The guitarist smiled sheepishly on seeing Don Chepe. "Good afternoon, *patrón*," he said, in a thick drawl, and was echoed by the others in the group.

"Good afternoon, Eufronio," Don Chepe said, surveying the men one by one. He pointed at the guitar. "Don't let our presence interrupt you."

"We were singing a few songs," the guitarist said, in his phlegmatic drawl. He was darker than his companions and had a bloodstain in one eye that gave him a cunning look. "Just to pass the time, *patrón*."

Don Chepe turned to the small boy with the hat over his eyes, whose attention had wandered to an emaciated dog by his feet. "And you, *muchacho*, how are you called?"

The boy reared back his head and grinned. "They call me *Nigua*, boss, because I'm no bigger than a louse."

"So it appears. And to which family do you belong?"

"No one's, *patrón*. My father got knifed in a fight and my mother went to another finca and left me with my brother Eufronio." He clutched the guitarist's sleeve and looked down at the dog. "Mongrel. Stop licking my toes, mongrel."

"I am all the family he has," Eufronio said, hunching his shoulders in resignation. But his smile was sly.

"Why haven't you brought him to me before?" Don Chepe

said. "Why isn't he in school?"

Eufronio shrugged. "I think you'd better ask him, *patrón*."

Before Don Chepe could ask the boy looked up with his papaya grin. "I went to the school one time, but it didn't result very well."

"And why didn't it result very well?"

"Because the other boys fuck me," he said, in a sing-song voice, and showed us a gap in his mouth were two front teeth were missing.

Don Chepe roared. The *mozos* raised their eyes for the first time and chuckled softly among themselves, only Eufronio's dark face remained somber. Don Chepe instructed him to bring his brother to the house the following morning, adding that he would see to it that he was placed with a group of boys who would not dare "fuck" him.

"By the way, what was he singing?"

"Only a simple song, *patrón*," Eufronio said. "Nigua likes to sing." There was a restless shuffling in the group. Several men averted their faces.

"Is that true, Nigua?"

The boy nodded. "Yes . . . it's a good song, and the *muchachos* pay me one cent each if I sing it for them." He reflected a moment. "The pure truth, I don't like it so much. It is too long—"

I thought Eufronio pressed his knee on Nigua's shoulder just then, but I could not be certain. In any case, he fell silent.

"Why don't you sing us a little of this song?" Don Chepe said. "The three of us here will pay you fifteen *centavos* apiece."

Nigua looked to his brother for permission, but Eufronio's face had turned to stone. He turned to Don Chepe, who smiled as he dug in his pockets for a coin. "All right," Nigua said, and he began to sing.

After the first two verses I understood the uneasiness of the men. The song was a topical ballad of a type that has been popular in Guatemala since colonial times. It is made up of as many as forty or fifty stanzas strung together around a political or social theme and sung to a simple refrain. The ballads have nearly as many authors as they have stanzas, and new ones are tacked on as they make their way around the countryside. Their tone is usually satirical and their language nearly always bawdy. This ballad was both. Beginning with the "benevolent dictator" Jorge Ubico's abdication in 1944 it gave a vivid and highly barbed account of Guatemala's political fortunes over the past two-and-a-half decades. The opening stanzas excoriated the brief but bloody rule of Federico Ponce, who "threw coals in the revolutionary bonfires" with his greed and his despotic excesses, and went on to praise Juan José Arévalo's "Spiritual Socialism," which had paved the way for agrarian reform and the promise of "peasant liberation" under Arbenz. There followed an extended lament over the defeat of Arbenz by Castilla Armas and his *"gringo patrones,"* Dulles and Eisenhower. Armas's successors, Ydígoras Fuentes and Peralta Azurdia were given short shrift as "the Clown President" and "the puppet colonel of the United Fruit" who, when fed U.S. dollars, passed out green bananas that ripened into more dollars and so on in an unending cycle. The current office-holder, Mendez Montenegro, was dispatched as a "left-handed rightist" who hadn't the "eggs" to stand up to the military. The ballad climaxed with a tribute to "the bearded liberator across the seas" and his counterparts in Guatemala, "our guerrilla brothers in the Rebel Armed Forces who will come down from the mountains one day and fulfill the promises that were made to the common people."

Don Chepe had listened impassively throughout most of the ballad, smiling at some references and chuckling outright at the more colorful epithets. But he blanched visibly when agrarian reform was first mentioned, and he looked cold sober by the end. Gustavo never cracked a smile.

It had been evident from the start that Nigua had learned the ballad by rote, although he sang the thirty-odd stanzas in perfect Spanish and not in his clipped Indian accent. As he sang in his reedy soprano his attention had strayed to the dog, then to the rim of his hat, and from there to the buckles of Don Chepe's boots, which he fondled with his toes.

In a level voice Don Chepe asked Eufronio where Nigua had learned the song.

"I don't know, *patrón.* I think from someone in the village." He did not avert his eyes, as before.

Nigua gave him a puzzled look.

"Who taught you the song, son?" Don Chepe asked gently, pressing his shoulder.

Nigua turned again to his brother, then back to Don Chepe. This time he did not grin. "Where are my fifteen cents, *patrón?*" He stretched out a brown hand.

Smiling, Don Chepe pulled out three silver coins from his pocket and placed them carefully on his palm. "Bring him to the house tomorrow morning," he said, turning to Eufronio. "Don't forget. I'll be expecting both of you."

The sun dipped into the sea as we made our way through the *cafetal.* Dusk, which comes rapidly on the coast, seemed to be racing us to the house. Don Chepe's spirits had deserted him. The long walk and the encounter with the men had dulled the effects of the wine, and a lifting breeze cleared our heads. He limped along in sullen concentration, muttering under his breath.

"I will have to get rid of him," he said finally. "I will have to get rid of Eufronio. He's a bad influence on my men . . . It can't be helped," he added, as if to settle the matter within himself. "In March, after the harvest, he goes." He straightened his shoulders and walked with a firmer gait.

Stars were out by the time we reached the gravel path; all that remained of the sunset was a faint lavender arch over the sea. Don Chepe waved excitedly at someone sitting on the veranda.

"Ah there she is. She has come down from her bath to greet us."

Teresita sat all alone by the wicker table, mending a skirt. A ring of moths and winged roaches danced about the light bulb over her head.

"So!" Don Chepe greeted her, lumbering up the stairs, "—her royal highness condescends to honor us with her presence!" Teresita looked up from her sewing and smiled indulgently at his little joke. In the dim light of the veranda her features seemed as fine as her father's, and her complexion was the rich lustrous brown of sapodilla wood. Her long freshly washed hair was wrapped in a blue and white bandana.

"Much pleasure," she said, when Don Chepe introduced me, and extended a limp hand. She acknowledged Gustavo's greeting with a light tilt of her head.

Don Chepe settled down with a loud sigh and slipped the goatskin *bota* from his shoulder. Gustavo and I declined his invitation to lead off a fresh round, so he gulped down most of the remaining wine on his first attempt.

"That skirt she's mending," he said, smacking his lips and pointing his cane—"that is one of the skirts she brought back from Sevilla. She is altering the hem so she can wear it for the arts festival in Antigua next April. Isn't that so, Teresita?"

"Yes, Don Chepe," she said, without removing her eyes from the needle.

"It is a pity you won't be here to see her dance," Don Chepe said. "She has become a very good dancer, although she is still a little timid. In Sevilla, during the fair, she would not perform in the pavilions even though she could dance the *Sevillanas* as well as anyone there. Do you remember, daughter?"

Teresita nodded, and Don Chepe raised his inflamed eyes to the ceiling, smiling at the memory and shaking his head. He passed the wine and Gustavo and I each took our turns—hurried ones, for neither of us was thirsty. And then Don Chepe drank again. When he'd had his fill he thrust the wineskin in Teresita's face, but she recoiled from it as if stung.

"Teresita doesn't drink wine." He sighed. "It is one of my great disappointments. She once tried a little in Sevilla but—do you remember, Teresita?—it didn't agree with her." He laughed. "She made the mistake of mixing her wines . . . *tinto y blanco*. It didn't agree with her at all." Again he laughed, a shrill, mirthless cackle. "I had to carry her to our rooms, stiff leg and all, and ask the lady of the house to help me put her to bed. You do remember *that*, eh Teresita?" He slapped his knee and bent over the table, convulsed.

Teresita gave him a look of undisguised fury.

"That-is-why-she-won't-drink-wine," he gasped, out of breath, and sat up to wipe his eyes. His laughter subsided as abruptly as it began, and he even succeeded in looking momentarily shame-faced.

Maria came in to announce that dinner would be ready in fifteen minutes, but Don Chepe cut her short and sent her scuttling for more wine. The macaw followed her along the rail, calling her name.

After she brought the fresh *bota*, Don Chepe drank steadily and rambled on in a husky monotone about the Sevilla of his youth, and about Teresita. His eyelids drooped, wine oozed from his lips, and his words began to slur and trip over one another. Teresita plied her needle without pause, glancing now and then in our direction but never once meeting our eyes.

"I am getting rid of Eufronio," Don Chepe said. "He teaches Bolshevik songs to my men. I will root him out like a weed—Eufronio and all his henchmen."

Teresita looked up from her sewing and locked eyes with Don Chepe.

"Ramiro is responsible," Don Chepe said, his voice rising. "Ramiro poisoned their hearts against me."

"They killed two planters yesterday," Teresita said, evenly. "They killed two planters yesterday afternoon in San Marcos. They drove up to their finca with machine-guns, tied their hands behind their backs and cut them down like two rats."

"I will root them out, you hear me?" Don Chepe shouted. "I will root them all out." He squirted a thin stream of wine into his mouth, wiped off the excess with a swipe of his hand and banged it hard on the table. "Your uncle Ramiro is responsible for this. He poisoned their hearts against me."

Teresita's cheeks flushed, and she laughed, a high mocking cackle like her father's. "Ramiro and I are one," she said. "His blood and mine are the same."

"Then I will root you out too!" he roared, and banged his hand on the table again.

"Ramiro is coming," Teresita said, in a low voice. "He is coming to take me away."

Don Chepe's jaw dropped, but he quickly recovered. A drunken grin disfigured his face. "Your uncle doesn't have the balls to set foot in this finca again. If he does, I'll finish the job I began with

the horsewhip. I will shoot down your uncle Ramiro like a rabbit."
He leaned toward her. "Like a rabbit, do you hear?"

Teresita laughed again, and rose to her feet. "You could not hurt Ramiro with your horsewhip, and you will never kill him with your bullets. It is he, Ramiro, my own blood, who is coming to kill you. He will cut you down with his machete, like a dead vine." Teresita started up the stairs, her face inflamed as if she had been drinking.

"I will kill him, do you hear?" Don Chepe shouted after her, but his voice was hoarse and barely audible above the screeching of the macaw, which signaled Doña Tomasina's approach.

"Dinner is served, Don Chepe," she said. She looked at each of us without expression, and withdrew.

Teresita did not come down for dinner, which was tense, silent, strained almost beyond endurance by Doña Tomasina's wordless padding to and fro with the dishes. I was relieved when it was over and Don Chepe saw us to the car, tottering unsteadily with two bottles of *manzanilla* under his arm. He said one was for Gustavo's father and the other to give us sustenance during the night. "It will be a long drive. If you finish both bottles wire from the nearest town and I will send another."

As Gustavo backed the car out of the driveway I looked up and saw Terresita's silhouette through an upstairs window. I waved to her but she made no response. She was not looking down but out beyond, toward San Marcos.

Born 1934, Victor Perera is a citizen of Guatemala with residence status in the USA. He has been a reporter, editor, university lecturer and author of articles, stories and essays. At last contact he was researching and writing a book on the Lacandon Mayas of Chiapas, Mexico.

"An elephant stops and everyone jumps
to religious conclusions!"

The Elephant Stop

BY G.S. SHARAT CHANDRA

A royal elephant causes chaos.

SEVEN days before the commencement of the Dassara celebrations in the kingdom of Mysore, on its morning walk through
the city the royal elephant refused to budge beyond the corner of
the main bazaar street on the one side and the temple of Kali on
the other. There was no explanation to its behavior. It looked
happy and swung its trunk jauntily as always except it did not wish
to move beyond the shade of the gulmohur tree which thanks to
its chance existence at the very spot provided enough shade until
the matter was looked into. The chief mahout arrived, examined
the beast, particularly the legs. He coaxed it with a sack of
coconuts. The elephant grabbed as many coconuts as it could,
trumpeted its glee but stayed steadfast. People gathered. The
mahout ordered guards and departed in haste. Now there's nothing unusual about an elephant stopping in its walk anywhere it
pleases. They have sturdy legs and sleep while standing. But

unlike circus elephants trained to do awkward manoeuvers for the titillation of the public, the royal elephant is trained by masters in the art of mammal etiquette. Its behavior in public is crucial to the dignity and decorum of the royalty. The present elephant's great grandfather was famous for its impeccable manners and it had expired one day with its head turned to the wall in such a graceful manner it looked as if it was napping. Rigor Mortis set in and it had taken a half dozen mahouts and as many poles to roll the corpse down.

The Dassara celebrations were only days away and the royal astrologer had predicted everything would go smoothly. News of the elephant's behavior spread to the palace. The Master-in-Charge of the Dassara celebrations came to inspect the situation. He was a shrewd man. He did not wish to cause any anxiety to the King before he was certain there was no alternative. He sent for the veterinarian, who examined the elephant with a stethoscope, ordered some pills to be given three times daily in sugar-cane juice. A chapra was built over the elephant's head with bamboo poles and thatched with palms. Over the roof the purple canopy with the royal insignia was hoisted. The elephant's personal sweeper, washer and manicurist were posted. More guards arrived to secure the area. The elephant stood majestically flapping its ears, swinging its well groomed tusk this way and that.

Next morning it became clear the elephant would not move. Maharaja Chamadharma, King Chum to his British friends at the Race Course club, sat with a hangover. He had missed the auspicious Tuesday morning puja to the royal deity and worried about a possible curse. Perhaps he would slip while playing tennis. King Chum's father, Raja Raja Verma, King Verm to his friends in the Buckingham palace, neglected rituals so badly on the first day of his first Dassara, that he tripped on the footstool to the throne and broke his knee cap. He limped somewhat for the rest of his life. Chamadharma sent for the royal astrologer. The queen simply said, "It's my husband's karma catching up! His sordid affairs with English women and whisky!"

It was common knowledge the King and the Queen did not sleep together. Their marriage was one of politics. She was plump, superstitious, interested in embroidery, nuts and sweets and gossip. The King was trained in a school for princes in Paris. They had no issue.

The royal astrologer examined the pachyderm, inquired about the direction of its head when it came to a standstill, made his calculations. The elephant had stopped because of some spiritual static that must have occurred at the intersection. The Kali temple nearby could be the source. The animal with its extra sensory perception must have seen something evil. He would prepare an amulet for the elephant and offer special puja to goddess Kali.

The elephant did not move.

By the evening of the third day, the elephant stop had become a point of public interest. Women found it a god-sent opportunity to worship. They offered it coconuts, jaggery and rice, brought their children for a chance to stomp on its droppings. But the droppings were sacred and were removed by the sweeper before the children had a chance. A wagon stood nearby, ready to cart off the containers for burial in the royal grounds. Villagers parked their bullock carts causing traffic jams. The motors and city bus were detoured to other streets. An enterprising brahmin saw an opportunity and put up a coffee stand. Hawkers with fruits, vegetables, flowers appeared. The town newspaper carried headlines with route directions to the elephant stop.

In the palace there was a steady mounting of panic. Unless the elephant got back to the palace, there was no Dassara. If it were left to Chamadharma, he would have had it tied up and brought back in a lorry. But that would have caused unimaginable chaos in the palace and in the mind of the public. The beast was sacred. It was the incarnation of God Ganesha. No force could be used on its will. Chamadharma had enough trouble keeping his karma within manageable limits.

The astrologer made more calculations and revealed that the problem was more complicated. The entire royalty had to purify themselves. He narrated from an old text that many years before the coming of the Mughals and the British, the then Maharaja of Mysore had issued an edict at the very spot the elephant had stopped. The edict spoke of the King's belief that elephants are the most noble beasts on earth. He had a marble statue of the then royal elephant erected next to it. The present royal elephant had remembered both the edict and some wrong doing to itself and fallen into a trance.

Therefore it was necessary to do the following. First the King should undertake pilgrimage to the Tirumalai hills. The Queen and the courtesans should fast for three days. The palace should offer silver and food to all the brahmin purajis of the kingdom. Further the courtesans should gather at the elephant stop on the fifth day, worship and bathe it under the supervision of the royal astrologer. The King thought the whole thing a farce. An elephant stops and everyone jumps to religious conclusions! What if he celebrated the Dassara without it! What if he substituted another who looked exactly alike! He asked if there were any restrictions on the type of his travel. There were none. He ordered his plane to be prepared. The queen welcomed the purifications. Fasting would be good for her body and mind. She had been eating too many sweets. The courtesans did not like any of it. But they existed under the royal patronage. The had to do what they were told.

The king left immediately, with his personal assistant and dress boy. The royal plane was seen heading in the direction of the hills. The courtesan march to the elephant stop became the talk of the town. The local newspaper carried stories on each of the seventeen courtesans with pictures. Literary luminaries contributed articles on the events and the role of religion in human conduct. The day the courtesans began their procession, the entire route was jammed with people. The radio supplied running commentary. The procession was a solemn affair since the courtesans, most of them in their middle ages, were weak without food. The senior of them led the group. She was sixty-five and had to rest under an umbrella every few steps. The royal orchestra accompanied the group with slow, pensive dirges. When the courtesans arrived at the elephant stop, the astrologer instructed the senior courtesan to shave the elephant's navel area and to apply a concoction of herbs. The others went around the beast touching its trunk, its belly, its tail, chanting forgiveness. People were touched. Finally, the courtesans washed the elephant with jugs of sacred water, pouring it over designated areas of its body to the chanting of the astrologer. The royal orchestra played mournful tunes from Hindu movies then settled back to their favorite medley from the follies.

The elephant lifted its trunk and salaamed repeatedly.

The sixth day came. The King returned looking pale and exhausted. He had pondered over the absurdity of the whole situation en-route to the hills and had the pilot change the course to Bombay. He had spent his time in the Taj Mahal hotel. The queen lost three pounds. She moved through the palace with the swiftness of an impala, her face beaming with religious virtuosity.

Exactly five hours before the morning of the Dassara, the elephant released a tremendous blast of gas and abruptly moved from the elephant stop.

Born 1935 in Mysore, India, G.S. Sharat Chandra was educated as a lawyer and taught law until 1967 when he made the decision to abandon law for literature. He teaches English literature and creative writing; he has taught at universities in several countries. His short stories and poetry are published around the world. His story "Jamal the Constable" appeared in SSI No. 9.

"The 'Flower of the West' Festival is primarily a beauty contest."

The Stranger

BY MICHAEL FOLEY

As Thoreau said: Beauty is where it is perceived.

IT was a time of great activity in the town. The "Flower of the West" Festival was about to begin and the citizens were busy with preparations. Fresh bunting and streamers were going up, tradesmen were fussing over displays and a noisy loudspeaker van was touring the streets. Those with nothing to do congregated outside the "Flower of the West" offices.

So it was that no one noticed a strange arrival at the station. The train had been standing for some time and the sole first-class traveller was leaning back in his seat smoking a cigar. Two things happened almost at once. The loudspeaker van swept by the station advertising the festival, and the train began to pull out of the station. On hearing the announcements the man at once became alert and jumped to his feet. A look of great excitement came on his face and he flung away his half-finished cigar. Then he began seizing items of baggage and throwing them out of the window. When this was completed he opened the door, braced himself (for the train was now moving at speed) and jumped out on to the platform, falling and rolling over several times before climbing to his feet, breathless but apparently unhurt.

This was the man who came to be known as The Stranger.

Some time later he was seen at the reception in the Commercial Hotel. He was interested in the Festival, he would like a room overlooking the square. All were intrigued by this eccentric, dressed in a tweed suit and heavy cape, looking for all the world like an English gentleman of some forty years earlier, his luggage consisting of a large suitcase, an empty wooden bird cage and what appeared to be an enormous leather rifle case.

"That's a brave day now," Con O'Neill, the owner, attempted conversation. The Stranger did not reply.

"Ye'll not find much to shoot around here," Con pursued, glancing suggestively at the case. The Stranger looked at him and gave a short harsh laugh. Then he went to his room, refusing to let anyone touch either the cage or the case.

News of The Stranger spread swiftly and his comings and goings were widely reported. In the course of the evening he was seen in the Athletic Bar, Owney Martin's, the American Bar, Hugh's Bar, the XL, and The Shamrock Lodge. Finally he turned up once more in the Commercial Hotel which boasted the finest lounge in the town. This was where the business community met, men like James "Oregon" Duffy, Big Bendy, the garage owner, and Myley Conaghan, the grocer and gent's outfitter. These were important people, men with daughters at convent schools and big houses "out the road." Yet here, as elsewhere, The Stranger sat alone, rejecting all attempts at conversation. Repulsed and baffled, the regulars fell back on conjecture.

"Maybe he's travelling for something new," Myley Conaghan suggested. "Some kind of swanky cigars or something."

At this point Slabbery Mickey came into the room. This was the town simpleton, so named because of his drooling mouth. His appearance was extreme—tattered clothes, hair brutally shorn and standing on end—but his eyes were shining with excitement at the commotion of the Festival. He came into the center of the room and looked round with a pleased, expectant air. Jimmy Oregon took this opportunity to approach The Stranger, who was still at a table of his own although the room was now quite crowded.

"Wait till you see this," he said, giving The Stranger a familiar nudge, "this is Slabbery Mickey. His mother took him to Sligo once and he ran away and stole three packets of liquorice allsorts out of Woolworths. The judge asked him why he did it and says Mickey, 'Ah needed big money fast.' The judge said his attitude was very distressing and gave him six months. Didn't know he was simple, ye see."

And Jimmy Oregon placed his hand on The Stranger's shoulder and leaned over him, helpless with laughter. Myley Conaghan was addressing Slabbery Mickey.

"Here Mickey, give us a bit of French. Come on."

"Hokey bokey. Hokey bokey cokey."

"Good man, Mickey. And what about a bit of Spanish?"

"Atty batty watty. Batty atty watty."

Mickey beamed with pride and there was applause from the little group at the bar and from others who were being drawn into the spectacle. Aware of an audience, Myley jumped to his feet and, catching Mickey by the shoulder, addressed those watching.

"Now Mickey's going to lift the bar—aren't ye, Mickey?" This was Mickey's speciality. He nodded eagerly and crouched down on the floor, putting one arm round each side of the bar. Then he began to strain, grimacing with effort, veins standing out on his forehead, sweat running down his face in streams. The bar did not move but Mickey's arms gradually moved up to shouts of "Rise her up, Mickey" and "Good man yourself." Eventually his arms reached the top and he left off, panting happily.

"Good on ye, Mickey!"

"Sound man!"

Everyone was watching now and The Stranger had full attention when he rose and walked to the bar.

"Michael needs a drink." This was taken as a witticism and there were loud cries of agreement. These died away when The

Stranger turned, face white with rage, eyes blazing a look that "went through ye like a dose of salts" as Myley Conaghan afterwards put it. A drink was quickly poured and presented to an uncertain Mickey.

"And now," The Stranger turned to Myley, "I understand you're a gent's outfitter."

"That's correct, yes."

"I would say that Michael needs a new suit." And here he had such difficulty that there were long pauses between each word, "For the Festival, you know. Italian style B, with pencil legs and cloth-covered buttons."

Myley's mouth dropped open in amazement. "A bum-freezer, ye mean?"

The Stranger gripped the bar with white hands.

"I . . . mean . . . Italian . . . Style B. Make . . . a . . . note . . . of . . . that."

"Yes . . . yes," Myley dithered, patting his pockets hopelessly. Finally someone handed him a scrap of paper and a pen and The Stranger swept from the room leaving behind some minutes of total silence and then the greatest hubbub the Commercial Hotel had ever known.

At around this time it was learned that The Stranger had adopted a mongrel dog, which he had christened Padraig Pearse. Also Sadie the maid discovered that the great rifle case contained not a weapon but several pairs of soiled underpants.

The consternation was greater than ever.

Then a strange thing occurred in the Commercial Hotel. Big Bendy was telling Myley Conaghan a good one.

"Wait till you hear the crack, Myley," he was saying. "Ye know the eldest boy, a very serious customer, always his nose in a book? Well, I sent him out for a good winter coat. Sent him down to your place and, wait till you hear, didn't the eejit go into the Black Man's by mistake."

"Oh he wouldn't be the first," Myley Conaghan was answering, "Many's a one made the same mistake—sure doesn't it look much the same on the outside."

But they both fell silent when The Stranger came into the room in the company of Biddy Keenan. Biddy Keenan was a tinker. She stalked across the room, insolent and disdainful, practically flouting her shawl and rags. The Stranger followed close behind, never taking his eyes from her, ignoring Myley Conaghan who plucked his sleeve and muttered that the suit was "coming on rightly."

Everyone fell silent and it was then that the incident occurred. A ragged newsboy, obviously an old enemy of Biddy's, put his head round the door and, cupping his hands to his mouth, shouted as hard as he could.

"Biddy, Biddy,

Wi' the big wooden diddy!"

At once Biddy's hauteur changed to animal rage. She swung round and crouched, baring her teeth in a snarl.

"Get outa that, ye huer's welt," she screamed and flung an empty bottle with vicious speed. But the urchin was faster still, disappearing long before the bottle burst above the door. At once Biddy recovered her composure, grinning broadly and moving on to a vacant table. The Stranger, who had watched all this with complete calm, at once rushed ahead and held out her seat. While Biddy adjusted her shawl and glared around triumphantly, The Stranger went to the bar for drinks.

"A large whiskey and a Thunderball, please." Con O'Neill gaped helplessly. "Gin and port and a dash of lime," explained The Stranger with great tolerance.

The "Flower of the West" Festival is primarily a beauty contest. There is a large and growing list of side attractions but the principal feature is the "Flower of the West" final in the big marquee on the Saturday night. The "Flower of the West" finalists line up on stage and each is presented by her sponsor, the winner being chosen by popular acclaim, a method bitterly rued by the committee on this occasion.

The only entry restriction is that the Flower's parents must have been born in the west of the country. This leaves a fairly wide range and as well as local girls there are Liverpool Flowers and New York Flowers and Chicago Flowers and so on. It is the custom for the Flowers to present themselves to the people in a motorcade through the town on the Friday before the final. Each car contains one Flower and is boldly marked "Chicago Flower," "Glasgow Flower" or whatever. There is much cheering and honking of horns—it is a fairly informal affair.

On the Friday afternoon of this festival the cars were lining up in the town square when a most peculiar sight was seen. A tractor driven by The Stranger drove up to the end of the procession and pulled in behind a giant Ford Estate draped with a banner inscribed "Winnipeg Flower." On the back of the tractor stood Biddy Keenan, dressed as usual except for a huge sash bearing the legend "The Wild Flower." This new arrival was greeted with a noisy outburst of clapping and cheering. The Stranger remained at the wheel and gave every sign of joining the motorcade.

The committee were hopelessly divided. Con O'Neill was for cutting him out—he was "making a reel of the whole thing." But others were against interference—the parade was for fun, they argued. Any attempt to curtail the fun would rebound on their own heads. They would be accused of "taking it thick."

In the end the latter counsel prevailed and The Wild Flower was allowed to take part, which she did in fine style, accompanied by an excited Padraig Pearse and an equally excited Slabbery Mickey, resplendent in his new suit. Several of her children were also there combing the pavements with cardboard boxes, droning: "Any money for de Wild Flower now, any money for de Wild Flower at all."

But would she enter for the final? This would really make a mockery of the town. A deputation was sent to The Stranger—James "Oregon" Duffy, Myley Conaghan and Con O'Neill.

They found him adamant. The Wild Flower had a beauty all her own. They might not be able to see this, he was sorry for them if they couldn't—but he for one could see it and would make sure it got a fair chance. He would enter her for the final. After that it was up to the people.

"Ye're makin' a cow's cock o' the whole thing," shouted "Oregon" Duffy in a sudden rage. At once Padraig Pearse rushed at his legs barking furiously.

"Easy boy. Down Patrick." The Stranger was calm, unruffled. "May I narrate a dream I had some time ago? An intensely personal experience but it may have some relevance here." And taking Padraig Pearse on his knee he began the following story.

"One night I was working late on some papers when I seemed to hear a whisper 'Come.' I turned round and there appeared a man who motioned to me. I followed him outside where he vanished, though I felt his breathing beside me. I found myself in the woods, wet branches and leaves slapping against my face. I walked till my legs were sore and wet to the knees. Finally we came to a dark round tower. Again I heard the whisper 'Come' and I entered, seeing him before me once more. I looked deep in his eyes and they seemed to reflect all the horrors he had seen in his life.

"Then I heard footsteps and a woman came in. She was poorly dressed and barefoot but her arms were pale and smooth, without a blemish. As I looked at her a happy feeling came over me.

" 'I must dry your clothes,' she said. They were indeed quite sodden now. Water was oozing out of my shoes. I did as she told me—took of my clothes and gave them to her. We went up a winding staircase and into a room with a vaulted ceiling. Not a ray of light penetrated the darkness.

" 'This is my bed,' she whispered. And then again 'Goodnight.' I tried to detain her but she faded into the air. Then my night became a fairy tale, a lovely golden memory. I was alone. The night was as thick and heavy as velvet. I was exhausted, my knees were shaking. I was in a daze. At last I lay back and fell into a deep sleep.

"In the morning I awoke in my own room. My clothes were at the foot of the bed but they were damp. My shoes were soaked through."

The Stranger paused for a long time, stroking Padraig Pearse who had fallen asleep in his lap. Then he resumed softly.

"As I now know the man was Slabbery Mickey and woman was Biddy Keenan."

The great marquee was crowded to bursting point. The situation was worse at the entrance, hopelessly blocked by scores of new arrivals and by the steady stream to and from the refreshment tent. A band was playing on the stage but few of the huge crowd were listening. All interest was centered on the contest to come and the merits of the finalists were hotly disputed. Feelings were strongest where the Wild Flower was concerned.

She had more supporters than expected, for news of her entry had spread and the last few days had seen a great influx of tinkers coming to support her. This influx had so alarmed the committee that they had considered abandoning the contest altogether. Then they had thought of banning The Wild Flower—but the tinkers would certainly "rise a row" if she didn't appear.

At last the entrance was closed off and the constest got underway. The finalists took their positions on stage, a special cheer greeting The Wild Flower. The sponsors took it in turns to introduce the Flowers. As usual the language was conventional in the extreme. There was much mention of "laughing colleens" and of "rosy red lips" and "snow white skin."

This was normally well received but tonight the audience were restless and ill-disposed to conventional praise. In fact the finalists were being discussed in openly physical terms. Some were praised as "good hoults," others scorned as "cauld curts" and the Winnipeg Flower, by all appearances a very serious girl, had been terribly upset by a loud suggestion that there were cobwebs on it.

The committee was of course alarmed by this increasing rowdiness. But it all ceased abruptly when The Stranger rose to speak. It was obvious that, here at last, the emotions were sincere. Indeed his feelings were so intense that he had difficulty in speaking at all. His voice was scarcely above a whisper and yet the silence was so complete that he was clearly heard at the back of the marquee.

His sentiments were as unusual as his manner. He spoke of the beauty of ordinary things, how in the rush and bustle of our lives we tend to undervalue all that is most precious. Rarely do we have time to reflect and often it takes a complete stranger to open our eyes to the beauty around us. In this very town such a beauty existed.

And he told them a moving story—how one day he had gone to

the public gardens to see the flowers. There were the "fat complacent chrysanthemums" and the "proud, righteous tulips." He spoke of the beds with their "well nourished soil" and their "careful designs" and their "perfect unbroken ranks" and he told how he had gone out from that garden and seen a single lowly dandelion sprouting from a crack in the pavement. Although it was a crowded thoroughfare he had no choice but to make his feelings known.

"I had no choice," The Stranger said, "The terrible poignancy of that flower tore a cry from my lips."

When he sat down there was silence for a full minute. Then there was uproar. The outcome was certain now—The Wild Flower had it easily. The band came back on and the refreshment tent, entirely empty for so long, was hit by a tidal wave of customers. There was laughter and dancing and the center of attraction was the triumphant Biddy Keenan. She was "swizzed" in the center of the floor by a succession of laughing young men. Then she was carried shoulder high twice around the marquee. Then she was installed on a throne on the stage.

Finally The Stranger was called on for another speech and only then was it discovered that he was nowhere to be seen. No one had seen him leave and a search around the tents revealed nothing. There was a growing uneasiness and an anxious party, headed by Slabbery Mickey, set off for the Commercial Hotel.

What they found was a room with no people or belongings, only a mongrel dog whining and scratching an empty bird cage.

It was some years later. A small group of friends, James "Oregon" Duffy, Big Brendy and Myley Conaghan were on their way from the Atlantic Bar to the Commercial Hotel. As always they were marvelling at how much had still to be learned about that momentous Festival week. James "Oregon" Duffy was particularly engrossed, staring at the ground, not taking much part in the conversation, a look of great amazement on his face. Suddenly he stopped them all dead in their tracks and burst out,

"Did yese know Patick Pearse was a bitch?" Myley and Big Brendy were dumbfounded.

"What was that?"

"What?"

"Padraig Pearse was a bitch. Sadie the maid told me. His mongrel, ye remember. It was a bitch—but he called it Padraig Pearse."

Big Brendy and Myley were no less amazed.

"I didn't know that now. That's a good one."

"That's a new one one on me too. Boys-a-boys-a-boys."

And the old friends continued on their way.

Born 1947 in Derry, Northern Ireland, Michael Foley was educated there and at Queens University, Belfast. He is a former coeditor of The Honest Ulsterman. *For several years he wrote a satirical column for the political review* Fortnight. *His short stories and poems appear in magazines and anthologies. At present he is teaching in London.*

" 'We drove him away,' he said. 'We did it.' "

Marry A Greek

BY JOY COWLEY

The culture gap packs a wallop.

THERE was no room in the house for his grief. It was too much, a pain too big to be contained within walls, and yet there was nowhere else he could go. He walked from one doorway to another and back again, turning abruptly like a bear in a cage, while June followed him, asking the same questions.

"Why didn't they send a wire? They're not that poor, surely. Nick? Why a letter? Couldn't they phone? Couldn't they at least cable?"

He stopped in the middle of the kitchen, shaking his head to avoid the extra pressure of her voice.

Not Papa. No, it was too soon. You hear that? Eh Papa? It can't happen yet. There is so much between us that hasn't been done.

He swung his arms uselessly at his sides.

I tell you, Papa, it isn't possible for you to be dead.

"When was it mailed?" asked June. "The postmark, Nick.

Have a look at the date. Darling? Please, the letter. Let me see it."

She opened his fingers and took the ball of blue paper from him. She flattened the page on the table, smoothing the creases between her hands, then leaned over it, her eyes only inches from the writing. Her hair fell forward hiding her face and her backbone showed in the gap between her jersey and her jeans. And suddenly Papa was there at her side, not to answer his questions, not to explain anything, but to stare at June's tight pants and nudge him and laugh.

"Nikis, my boy, she's beautiful. Beautiful. Ha ha, you're no bloody kiwi, son. You got the Greek eye. It's in the blood, huh? You know the choicest fruit and you know exactly when it is ripe. A beautiful peach, Nikis, you lucky dog."

June lifted her hair away from her face. "He must have been buried days ago," she said.

He nodded.

"There's no point in going over there now," she said. "If only they'd let you know in time."

"What's the difference?" he said. "I wouldn't have gone."

"Your own father's funeral?" She looked shocked. "Oh Nick. We could have managed—got a loan, sold the car, something. I could have gone back to work." She picked up the letter. "I don't understand them. Why didn't they let you know? They're only distant cousins. You—you're his son. Why? If they'd sent a cable we could have booked you on the first flight to Athens."

"It doesn't matter," he said. "Will you stop going on about it?"

Her mouth tightened. "Don't you care?" she asked.

He took the letter from her, folded it and put it in his shirt pocket, next to the pain that crowded his ribs. Breathing hurt him. Words hurt. He opened and closed his hands several times, looking for something to hold. He didn't know what. Then he started walking again. "What's the use of going to his funeral. I don't remember those people. They don't remember me. And *he* wouldn't know." He slapped his hands together. "When he was *alive,* that's when he needed me. Every letter, the same thing over and over, when are you coming, when am I going to see my grandson, when, when, when?"

She turned away from him. "Yes. Well. We didn't know he was going to have a heart attack, did we?"

He knew from the way she'd set her shoulders, that she was waiting for him to blame her. She was tense, ready with anger to defend herself, ready to shout her innocence.

She was so guilty in fact, that he had already forgiven her. He wouldn't have said a word, but Papa was there again, standing alone at the station with his old cardboard suitcase and raincoat, his gray hair set in brilliantine ridges.

Papa's small weakness that. Perfumed hair cream. Lavender, rose, carnation, essence of violets. His pillow cases always looked like old fish and chip papers.

The smell of Papa's hair drifted along the platform, greeting him long before he saw the outstretched hands.

"Nikis, Nikis, your father is a stubborn old fool. I was wrong to try and hold you and June. I know that now, huh? You are young. You have to move where your future is, your work, have your own house. For June, huh? She don't want the old house your Mama died in. So, it is time for me to give in, Nikis. You are the young bull, I am the old bull, and I give in to you. I sell the old place, come here to live with my son's family."

"To live, Papa? Here? But what about your friends?"

"So? I find new friends."

"But Papa, you know there is no Greek community here. You'll be lonely."

"Lonely? Nikis, Nikis, the whole world is my friend."

June was drying the dishes, her back to him. There was defiance in the way she flicked the towel over the breakfast plates. He put his hand on her shoulder and turned her round until she was forced to look at him. "We drove him away," he said. "We did it. If we'd given him a home, he'd never have gone back there."

"Don't take it out on me!" she snapped.

He shook her. "*We* did it to him! We turned him out."

She swung away from him. "You mean, I did. That's what you mean, don't you? That's what you're getting at."

He saw that she was close to tears. He shook his head. "No. No, I'm not. It was both of us. You didn't understand and I was weak."

She raised her hand quickly and for an instant he thought she was going to strike him. He blinked. But her arm came down again and instead she slowly tucked her jersey into her jeans. "Right," she said in a tight voice. "That's the last time you tell me I didn't understand. I wasn't going to say anything. I made a vow. Don't come between father and son, I told myself. Because that's just it, I did understand. Before we got engaged a girl at work warned me. 'Marry a Greek and you marry his whole family,' she said. 'You get them all, brothers, sisters, uncles, aunts, living on your doorstep.' But that didn't worry me. There was only your father. I was prepared for us to live with him. I knew that's what you'd want and I didn't mind. But at that stage, I didn't know what he was really like." She turned back to the bench. "I couldn't stand it!" she said, and she was crying. "The way he looked at me. And sometimes—once he did it in front of you, and all you did was laugh."

"What are you talking about?" he said.

She was sobbing.

"June?"

Tears were running down her face. "He was a dirty old man!" she shouted. "A bottom pincher! I hated him!"

He stared at her, unsure of her words. Then he held his hands out, cupped, as though some other explanation would fall from the air. "That's it?" he said at last. "That's the reason?"

"I didn't want to tell you," she said.

"No." He shook his head. "I don't believe it. You mean—that's what it was all about? But—but it was the biggest compliment he could pay you! Ooooh! Oh, you stupid, stupid bitch! You were beautiful. He loved your beauty. And this—this was why you hated him? God in Heaven, don't tell me. This was the reason I sent him away?"

She didn't answer.

"Oh—you—" The pain grew huge and choked him. "You poor, miserable bitch!" he said, and then he rushed out of the house, slamming the back door behind him.

He stopped by the gate and waited for a while, wondering if she would come out after him. She didn't. There was no sound at all from the house. He opened the gate and turned into the street, head down, hands in pockets. He wasn't going anywhere in particular, simply walking to free the pain in his chest and keep his thoughts moving.

There were a lot of people about, mowing lawns, cleaning cars, the things he usually did on a Saturday morning, and children rode bicycles over the footpath in front of him.

He was hardly aware of them, so real was Papa's face. Papa's voice.

For nearly two years, in fact ever since he left, Papa had been as distant as a faded photograph. Now, in death, he was so close and so big that he filled all earth and sky. Nikis. Nikis? His voice was louder than traffic. Nikis? And it didn't stop calling him.

There was a low stone wall outside the church. He sat, leaned forward against his knees, and stared at the cracked pavement. At the base of the wall, a few tufts of grass held a drift of confetti. He rubbed it with his heel. Rice was neater. The birds ate it. And they too, were God's creatures.

Papa believed in God. He talked about Him often as though God were a personal friend, benevolent, a bit of a rogue.

June didn't think much of Papa's religious views. "Why does he talk like that?" she said. "Who does he think he is?"

He got up quickly and started walking again. He needed a cigarette. He'd left his pack on the kitchen table, and he had no money with him. But there was the garage, the service station where he got his petrol. Dave Murdoch knew him. Dave wouldn't mind.

He crossed the street and walked round the cars that waited at the pumps. Saturday mornings were always busy here. He went into the office and leaned against the doorway. As he folded his arms he felt the crackle of thin paper in his pocket.

I know, Papa. I see it now. It's a joke. You're deliberately doing this to me. I haven't written for months so you think, aha, you'll teach me a lesson. Eh Papa? And right now you're in the tavern with your cronies, laughing your head off. The comedy of the year.

"Hello Nick." Dave Murdoch came in with a handful of money. "What can I do for you?"

"Have you got any—" He cleared his throat. "I'm out of cigarettes, Dave. I've left my cash at home."

"No problem." Dave opened the till, put the money in, shut it again. "They're up there. Help yourself."

"Thanks," he said. "I'll—I'll need matches too. Fix you up Monday."

"No hurry," said Dave. He was about to go out again, when he stopped and looked back, head on one side. "Anything wrong? Hey! Steady! You're not going to conk out, are you?"

"I'm all right." He held on to the doorway.

"You sure?" said Dave. "You don't look too hot."

"I'm sure," he said.

Dave came close, put his hand on his shoulder and peered at him. "Man, you'd better watch yourself. You're sick. I'll bet you a dollar to a doughnut, you're going down with that Asian virus."

He shook his head and closed his eyes against the rush of tears. Then the pain came out in big, ugly sounds. He couldn't speak. He put his head on Dave's shoulder and held on to him and cried.

Dave pulled him in from the doorway. "Hey, hey, come on. What's the matter? Nick? Cripes, man, what's happened?"

"Papa," he said against Dave's overall. "He's dead. Papa's dead."

"Your father?" Dave was trying to make him stand straight. "That's tough. I'm sorry to hear—look, Nick—"

"He's dead. And I killed him, Dave. I sent him away. I broke Papa's heart!"

"Nick, come on! Pull yourself together. You're not a kid. Nick? Stop it!" And Dave slapped him over the ear.

He stepped back. He blinked and put his hand against his face. "I'm sorry," he said.

"Wipe your nose," Dave said.

He had no handkerchief. He had to use his sleeve. "Sorry, Dave."

Dave pushed him towards a chair. "You can't go out like that.

You're suffering from shock. Sit down over there. Yeah, that's right. Now light a fag while I find out where they put my bottle. You sure got yourself churned up, haven't you?"

He sat beside the cluttered desk. "I'm sorry," he kept saying. "I'm sorry." He wiped his face again, but the tears still came, even though he was no longer crying.

"It's here somewhere," said Dave, on his hands and knees in front of a cupboard. "You can't find anything in this place. But I know I've still got it. Half a bottle of four star brandy."

"Thanks—I don't need a drink," he said. He lit a cigarette. His hands were shaking. "I should get back home. I left June—"

Dave was searching through shelves and drawers. "You're not going anywhere in that state," he said. "I know it's here. In this office. Hey—your father—isn't he the old fellow who went back to Greece?"

"Yes," he said.

"How did it happen? Heart?"

"Yes. It was very sudden."

"That's a comfort, anyway," said Dave. "I want to go like that. A long life and then—out like a light before you know what hits you. That's the story. It's hard on the family, but it's the best way. My old man died of cancer. Believe me, you wouldn't wish that on anyone. Ah, found it!"

"I'm fine now," he said. "I'd better go."

But Dave uncorked the bottle and picked up a cup ringed with coffee stains. "Get this inside you and you'll feel better." He put the cork between his teeth and filled the cup three-quarters full. "That should do the trick," he said, talking round the cork as though it were a cigar. "Drink up."

He sipped to oblige him.

"I got to give the boys a hand," said Dave. "You stay here where it's quiet. Just sit and take your time. Okay?" Then he went outside to the long line of cars and the noise of the pumps.

Oh Papa. Papa don't leave me.

He watched the cigarette burn down. His eyes were hot and swollen and his nose was running. He didn't want brandy. This wasn't the time for it. He put the cup down on some papers and covered his face with his hands.

Papa, I remember at the wedding you were such a little man, your head with its corrugated curls no higher than my shoulder. I could have picked you up with one hand. Then you started to grow and I began to shrink, smaller, smaller. Now you are as big as the world and I'm just a little kid, a baby. No Papa, I am nothing. My house is nothing. My new car is nothing. My wife, my son, my work.

You see, Papa, you lived on one side and she lived on the other. Neither of you could understand what it was like for me in the middle. I tell you, Papa, the man who stands in the middle has no country. No home. He is nothing.

He put out the cigarette and stood up, leaving the cup of brandy on the desk. The front of the service station was still jammed with cars. He went out the back way, through the workshop, into the yard, down the alley to the road.

He didn't remember walking home. Suddenly he was there in the kitchen with June standing at the bench, back at the beginning of it all.

But this time she didn't hammer him with questions. She looked at him for a moment, then came and put her arms round his waist, her head on his chest. He touched her hair. He was tired of saying he was sorry, but there was nothing else to say.

"I'll make you some coffee," she said.

"No," he said. "Stay with me."

But she pulled away. "Darling, you look awful. You've made yourself ill. I think I should call the doctor."

"Doctor?" He laughed. "What for? How can a doctor change anything."

"He'll give you a prescription," she said. "A sedative. You do need something, Nick."

He shut his eyes tight and put his hands over his head. "I need to be left alone!" he said.

She didn't answer. He heard her go into the next room and close the door.

He wished he hadn't said it. He was being stupid, childish. And his nose was running again.

One winter—long ago—he and Papa visited Mama's grave nearly every Sunday, and they both used to blow their noses on Papa's best white handkerchief.

When she died, he asked, "Is Mama an angel now, Papa?"

"Nikis, your mother was born an angel. When you're grown up you'll understand, all women are angels. It's the way God makes them—with big, loving hearts. Now a man, sometimes he has nothing to give a woman. But the woman, she can always give to the man. Remember that."

"Yes Papa, I'll remember."

He opened the sitting room door and held out his hands to June. "Please—"he said. But he stopped when he saw the quick light of fear in her eyes. He put his hands in his pockets. "I wouldn't mind some coffee," he said. "I—I feel very tired."

She relaxed and smiled. "It's the strain, darling," she said. "Why don't you go to bed for a while? Don't worry about the lawns. I can easily start the mower."

He stared at the carpet and shivered. "I'm cold," he whispered. "I don't know why. I'm so cold."

She patted him on the arm. "I'll turn on the electric blanket," she said.

Joy Cowley, successful short story writer and novelist, was introduced in SSI No. 2 with her tender story "The Silk." A gracious, enthusiastic person, Ms. Cowley started her career as a short story writer. Several years back she received a letter from a publishing house editor, who had just finished reading one of her short stories, asking if she had ever considered writing a novel. She hadn't, but soon did. Her work is also broadcast on radio programs.

"We've nothing to eat and my father
is going to give me away."

Rains

BY PIRA SUDHAM

Prayers and primitive sacrifices for survival.

"WHY do the grown-ups do things like that?" Dan asked, moving closer to his friend, Kum, who was still panting because they had been running along the hot sandy path.

Dan wanted to repeat the question but then Kum sat down on his heels, arms akimbo. Dan did so too, keeping close to his friend. Their elbows touched but the meager shade of the mango tree could not give them much comfort.

Kum's silence compelled Dan to be quiet. So Dan turned to the group of monks and the laymen of the village as they sat in the glaring sun. The monks were chanting in unison with their hands cupped in the manner of praying and their eyes closed while the villagers crouched in concentration.

Why must they perform such a ritual in the terribly hot sun? Dan wanted to ask but then he dared not disturb the solemnity of the gathering. In front of everyone there was a toad tied to a stake.

The animal was trying vainly to free itself, mortified by the human din and the exposure.

Dan was perplexed, his eyebrows curved into a silent question. Shifting uncomfortably, he once more searched Kum's face for explanation. Kum remained serious and mottled. The light and shade made an interplay on the boyish face.

"Why?" Dan tried to whisper, nudging his friend with his elbow.

Kum made a low grunting sound, then lapsed into his seriousness once more, staring intently at the monks and old men and women as if he was being stupefied by the awesome rite.

Dan's own grandmother and Kum's grandmother were among the people who were submitting themselves to the ritual. Missing were the school teacher and the Chinese shopkeeper. The latter had already packed up his shop and moved elsewhere since there was no more money to be made from the drought-stricken peasants.

Under this burning sun you could cook an egg in the sand, Dan was thinking, and why? Why do they make themselves so pitiful? The boy was moved by the sight of his grandmother as she swayed her perspiring, emaciated body to the rhythm of helplessness. Dan recalled what she had said to the members of the family, that if the monsoon did not come soon, it would mean famine. Her prophesy fell on all ears for it was what everyone was concerned about, in dread of. However, nobody commented or acknowledged her despair. So the old wizened woman lamented further saying that in her life she had never been through any year as bad as this.

The wind from the burning rice fields sheared hot and dry, carrying dust of two successive years of drought, breeding sorrow and fear, hunger and sickness.

The streams and the dams and wells were dry, and the earth cracked in millions of fissures. In the aridity of the wind there seemed to be mockery from the supernatural on the dignity and the significance of mankind. What could villagers do then but to torment themselves and the toad so that the supernatural, the spirits good or evil would take pity on them and so give them rain.

The rain-begging rite was their last hope when human resources failed. But Dan, being only six years old, did not understand the meaning of it. Nevertheless, he had been taught to respect the solemnity of the monks and the old people. He too sensed the despair prevailing in the sweltering air.

As if he could not bear the ceremony any longer, Kum gave up his serious pose. Taking Dan by the hand, he led the way, walking off, yet still in awe and silence. They went along the track where they had come, walking away disheartened, seeking comfort from each other by holding hands.

Hunger drove them from the emptiness of the fields into the woods to hunt for lizards. When they had caught a few of these reptiles, Kum made a fire and cooked their catch. After the scanty meal had been wordlessly eaten, Kum stopped being sulky. The heat waves rose high from the plain of salt pans and gray scrubs and endless mirages. Dan coughed the dust out of his parched throat which contracted from his effort to dare ask.

Lying under the shade of the tamarind tree, Kum answered:

"They tried to beg for rain from the lords, the spirits."

"Will it rain then?" Dan asked.

"It might," Kum said ruefully.

Dan scanned the skies for clouds which would give rise to their hope.

"Maybe in the evening," Dan hoped.

It was also Dan's attempt to comfort his friend. But Kum took on that expression of seriousness again, staring at the gray infinity distorted by the heat haze. He did not seem to mind the flies covering the wound on his left knee.

"The drought might be so bad that we don't have to go to school," Dan ventured after a long pause.

Could Kum be comforted not having to attend the village school under the gruelling supervision of the teacher who would flog children when they could not learn sums? So Dan's idea of going to school to face the teacher seemed more frightening than the famine.

"Aw, it's bad enough now," Kum groaned. "We've nothing to eat and my father is going to give me away."

Dan became tongue-tied with this information, at the thought that Kum would be taken away from the village by strangers whom one must call Dad and Mum. When Dan could speak, he said meekly:

"Maybe you could live with us."

Kum could not believe that was possible. "You don't know what the grown-ups would do," he said.

Then they left it at that, having touched on the gate of their own despair.

Days passed but no rain came. There was not even a faint thunder or the sight of rain-bearing clouds to raise hope.

Meanwhile, several families left the village for elsewhere where ponds and streams and rivers held water most time of the year and where the monsoon was regular and the earth yielded.

Rumors of those going to leave next spread fast; people called to one another saying goodbye. Ox-carts loaded with sad-eyed peasants and their children and possession rolled away, leaving dust and memories behind.

The village mourned its departed inhabitants. The soil turned sour. Loneliness and despair tinted the sounds of goodbye. In leaving, people reminded one another of the centuries of filial ties and kinship. The trembling voice of the aged sang back across the gulf of hopelessness. Would we ever see you again? they cried.

Meanwhile, the adults talked of the rites and sacrifices to gain mercy from the spirits.

For rain, life, the normal turn of the seasons.

Dan would rather suffer in place of his grandmother or of most old men and women for he felt sorry for them.

Perhaps they might let him join in some of the rites and make him a sacrifice. His suffering might help them to succeed and so prevent Kum from being taken away by strangers to a far-off place.

But Dan had not been included in the adults' suffering and responsibilities. He could only watch how the men killed an ox, a buffalo, a pig for their blood and flesh as the votive offering to the spirits at the village spirit house.

The rituals took on a more macabre air as the people became more desperate. The fatal twist of the knives, the mortal wounds, the deadly cries of the animals, and the flow of blood pointed to one thing: the men appeared despairingly savage.

But to no avail, except that the hearts were relieved by the primeval savagery and cruelty.

One day, Dan went off by himself.

The vastness of the arid landscape made the tiny boy more minute and singular.

Without Kum by his side, he began to be afraid of the solitude and the great expanse of the desicated plain. He halted several times, looking back towards the village.

Where Dan chose to sit was unprotected by any vegetation. Sitting cross-legged under the excruciating sun, he tried to pray, but since he had not been taught the art, his was only an imitation, following the manner of monks and old people he had observed. Closing his eyes, Dan swayed a little.

"Pity me. Oh spirits," Dan prayed.

The experience was both enthralling and fearful. For he, so insignificant and small, dared put himself up against the powerful.

Silence, which seemed to weigh heavily on him became a threat. The sun whipped him so mercilessly, that his head throbbed, and the perspiration ran down his face and torso.

"Pity me. Oh lords."

Gradually courage came back to him and helped him to expand wider. In departing from himself, Dan saw in his mind's eye the face of Kum, a face of seriousness and fear. Must Kum be taken away by strangers? Dan saw also himself coming home from the fields, hallooing and laughing, riding a water buffalo. The image of the old grandmother loomed: it was a picture of happiness when she turned to smile broadly at him while ploughing the paddies in a good year. Old as she was, she worked unabatedly provided that there was water enough to grow rice.

"Oh lords, have pity on Kum and grandma. Be merciful," Dan raised his voice.

The blazing sun kept beating at him, yet he prayed on. "Oh lords have mercy on grandma and all the old people. Grandma eats nothing; she is so old and boney. Her clothes are also old and tattered. Have pity on old people for they could not dig for yams and taro or chase grass-hoppers and catch lizards for food."

His endurance was that of a child's. Curiosity forced him to open his eyes to see the effect of his rite. But to his dismay the skies remained cloudless; there was no cool breeze to herald the approach of rain.

Heavy with disappointment the boy sighed and shifted. Perhaps his suffering was seen as a child's fancy, a mockery of the solemn and sacred reserved for monks and old men.

"My lords," Dan made another attempt, but no more words came.

The dehydrating heat of the sun was immense. He trembled at the thought that he would be consequently punished by the spirits for his fanciful action.

There seemed to be so much of the cynicism in life, the universal suffering, sorrow, the primeval bitterness and the futility of all things. Was it blood that pleased, or savagery and brutality and murder to be called for?

Now it was his own seriousness that frightened him so that he shuddered. But there was no way out now except to prove his sacrifice to the lords.

He must offer his blood to the lords.

The knife taken from his father's toolbox flashed in the noon sun.

Only then was he convinced that he would not fail for the sacrifice would be so immense that the lords would take pity on him and so yield rain.

But the sharp metal opened the wound deeper than intended on his wrist.

Dan winced with pain, throwing the instrument away. The flow of blood made him giddy, still he lifted the wounded hand towards the sun for the lords to see, till he fell.

Lying flat on his back, Dan tried to call out for help but could not. His throat was so dry, and he trembled seeing that darkness was descending quickly on him.

Yet he strained in sheer effort to hear any rumble of thunder that would mean rain.

Pira Sudham was introduced in SSI No. 1 with his short story "Toward the Unknown Region." Born 1942 in a remote village in northeast Thailand, he received his primary education there. During his second year at Chulalongkorn University, he won a scholarship to Victoria University in Wellington, New Zealand. A youthful-looking, charming person, he is attuned to several cultures. His stories are published in Thailand, Singapore, Hong Kong, the USA and other countries.

"That daddy of mine can do some violence . . ."

Lions, Kings and Dragons

BY MARGARET PERRY

**Shocking destruction under the banner
of parental concern.**

THE hour that ticked away was full of anxious sounds for Miss
Sandor. Her three o'clock pupil had not come, and she had done
nothing but sit in her living room to await J.T. She could have
practiced or cleaned a room, she reflected. Instead, she dreamed
and dozed alternately. Four o'clock . . . four-thirty. The boy did
not come.

J.T.'s father was still angrily opposed to the boy's music lessons.
"But I says to him," (Miss Sandor remembered that first day so
vividly: Mrs. Moses, fat, shiny, a creamy-brown face with the most
extraordinary pale green eyes, standing in her living room and
talking with a conviction of one who hates and loves with indomit-
able passion), "I says to him, 'It's my money an' I gonna see to it
he develops his natural talents.' After all, my daddy could sing to
make you weep. You shoulda hear him sing 'Jesus, Lover of My
Soul'," and her chest heaved so high that Miss Sandor thought

137

J.T.'s mother might break into song to prove she had transmitted the musical talent from father to daughter to grandson. But, sighing, she clasped J.T. to her side and hugged him protectively.

J.T. was eight—small, thin and wiry, colored the same hue as his mother. But his eyes were a brownish-yellow with small, dark pupils. Cat eyes, thought Miss Sandor. The two of them—proud, romantic mother, silent, watchful son—fascinated her so much she consented to the music lessons at a reduced rate (being extra careful, she felt, not to let Mrs. Moses suspect this) without hearing J.T. play, as Mrs. Moses put it, "lots of classical stuff he done picked up by lissening to the radio."

The financial terms and the time of lessons settled, Miss Sandor, on impulse, asked Mrs. Moses if she wanted tea.

"No mam', I guess we better git on home before that mean man of mine do. J.T., he got to play his piano before Mr. Moses show his face in the house."

"Oh, I see. Your husband must work very hard. I suppose he comes home tired and the sound of playing would disturb him."

"He do, he do work hard—but that ain't why J.T. don't play with him 'round. No need to make him remember J.T.'s likin' the piano, that's why, Lordy, no!"

"I'm sure it's not that bad," said Miss Sandor.

"If it was singin'—we all sings—his daddy wouldn't make no fuss." She shook her head. "But he say he ain't goin' to have no son of his playin' that fancy, sissy music."

Miss Sandor smiled. "He'll come round, you'll see."

"Humph." Mrs. Moses turned to leave. "You take care to teach J.T.—I'll see to Mr. Moses."

That had been six months ago. During the first few lessons Mrs. Moses came with J.T. and sat quietly in one corner, never uttering a word. Then J.T. came alone. After the first month of drills with scales, exercises and simple tunes, Miss Sandor one day, on impulse, asked him to play anything he liked because she recalled what his mother had stated the first day they met. J.T. grinned; then his expression grew solemn as he shifted himself a little to the right of Middle C. He closed his eyes, leaned back and began to play with light, rapid strokes. The shock of hearing him play the first movement of Mozart's "Concerto in C" left Miss Sandor faint with excitement. When J.T. finished, he turned and looked at her timidly.

"Oh, J.T., that was beautiful."

"Yessum."

"But you played it . . ." She wrung her hands. "How did you know it started on C?"

"Radio man says so. I done heard it a couple of times. That's how come I knows it by heart. I knows it all." He smiled. "You know it?"

She nearly wept. "Yes, yes. Look, J.T., we must . . ." Then she did cry, laughing at the same time the tears were falling. "Let's celebrate, J.T.," she finally managed to say. "How about some ice cream?"

"Yessum! I reckon I likes ice cream 'bout like I do Mozart."

He didn't know how to read music and resisted doing so until Miss Sandor told him he would eventually surpass her ability to play music for him to imitate. In his heart he didn't want to believe this; but he also knew she wouldn't lie to him. The regular music lessons were abandoned. He came nearly every day and practiced or was instructed between the lessons of other pupils. He often ate with her and while they ate, she would tell him stories of her travels around the world.

"You say London is larger than Washin'ton? I just can't see no town being that big!"

"You'll see it one day, J.T. One day you may be playing there."

"Oh, Lordy, my daddy will have a fit."

"J.T., you mustn't say that."

"True is true, my mama say."

"Still, people change."

"Yeah, like they gits meaner."

"Oh, J.T.!" She laughed and hugged him. "And think of us in Paris, too."

"Paris?"

"Yes. Paris, London, Vienna . . . Won't it be wonderful?"

This became their dream: to travel around the world as J.T. performed on the concert stage for an admiring public. Miss

Sandor began to dream of this nightly. In a while, in a while, they would go.

When he left her apartment, she always gave him a big hug. She loved to run her hand over the beady surface of his little head.

One day as they were sitting on the sofa, he leaning against her, she with an arm around him, both of them holding on to a large picture book she had bought him, he looked up and said:

"I wants to talk like you. Lissen to me read now."

He read a page of the story and tried to imitate her soft, Mid-Western accent. He sighed.

"Nope, ain't quite right. I gonna work on it, though. Trouble is, it ain't just the sound. I can work that out, like on the piano. Nope, I guess . . ." He looked at Miss Sandor and grinned. "I guess it's the words, gettin' them right, too."

"I can help you, J.T."

"That sure is askin' you a lot. My daddy might not take to that sort of carryin' on."

"Surely he couldn't object to any improvement you make."

"That daddy of mine can do some violence, Miss Sandor. It near 'bout kills him knowin' I comes here once a week."

"But, J.T., you come here nearly every day."

"Not that my daddy knows. Lordy, he'd cut me to little bits with that razor of his."

"Oh, J.T., you exaggerate."

"Told me so once."

"No, I'm sure he wasn't serious."

"I takes no chances. O, Miss Sandor, it's a big, long razor. He leave it hangin' in the bathroom."

"Now, now, let's not talk about it any more. Tell me, how do you explain being away from home every day, when you're here?"

"Tells him nothin'."

"But, J.T., that isn't right."

"Right for me, 'cause if my daddy knew he'd skin me alive." He sighed. "You see, Miss Sandor, he thinks I'm bad an' tough like the other kids. Mama say it just ain't my nature to be like that, an' she's right smart. Like you, Miss Sandor."

She gave him a squeeze. "Your mother is a very fine lady."

"My daddy say she got too many fancy ideas."

"I think she believes in the beautiful."

"Uh, huh. C'mon, Miss Sandor, let's finish readin' about the lions, kings an' dragons. Boy, they are the greatest!"

During the weeks that followed, it never occurred to Miss Sandor to wonder about the life J.T. led away from the world the two of them had created. She was not prying or curious by nature. Besides, there was a perfection about their relationship which required no investigation or explanation. Then, one day in May, Miss Sandor did what she had longed to do for months but hadn't dared: she attempted to invite J.T. to attend a concert with her.

Excited by the thought of the two of them seated side by side in Constitution Hall, impatient to ask him, Miss Sandor grabbed the telephone and dialed J.T.'s home number. Unexpectedly a gruff male voice answered.

"May I speak to Mrs. Moses?"

"She ain't here. Who's callin'?"

Miss Sandor hesitated. Then she told him her name because she decided he wouldn't recognize it.

"You that fancy teacher Lily done got for J.T.?"

"Why, Mr. Moses, I'm not sure I know what you mean."

"Uh, huh, you knows. First I heard your voice I thought you might be some ol' school teacher. But my girls an' J.T. ain't got nothin' but black teachers. They may be cultured—but not that cultured!" He laughed.

"Oh, Mr. Moses, you're just trying to flatter me."

"No, no don't think you right there. More like to flattern you." He laughed again, bitterly; then his voice stiffened. "I wants you to leave my J.T. alone, you hear?"

"I'm not sure I understand."

"So, that where he done got that 'I'm not sure' business. That the second time you done said that."

"There's nothing wrong in that, is there?"

"I 'spec' you don' think so."

"Naturally."

"Natcher'ly what?" The tone of his voice was brave and brassy.

"What you so proud of, lady?"

"Mr. Moses, I think you're being unfair."

"I don't give a damn what you thinks. You tryin' to ruin the onliest son I got."

"I would hardly call helping him develop his natural and extraordinary talent a ruination."

"Lady, you just as bad as him mama. She done call that boy somethin' most strange the other day. Say he's her black Mosart. Who he?"

"Wolfgang Amadeus Mozart—a child musical prodigy. She's absolutely right, you know."

"Name's just as bad, too. Julian Thaddeus. Who ever heard of a real man with names like that?"

"But they're beautiful names, Mr. Moses."

"You women is all alike."

"Mr. Moses, have you ever heard you son play?"

"I reckon I has. Some time or 'nother, but . . . Look, lady, we may be black an' not rich, but we ain't dirt poor."

"I never said anything to indicate you were." She was beginning to wonder if he were quite sane. "Mr. Moses, what are your specific objections to me?"

"You married?"

"No—but what in heaven's name has that to do with it?"

A low, guttural, ugly laugh pierced her ears. "Ain't good for J.T. to be hangin' round single ol' ladies."

"Really, Mr. Moses, I'm not that old!"

"You ain't? Hmm, now ain't that interestin'? What age you got?"

She giggled. "Past 21, I can assure you."

"That don't answer my question."

"Really, Mr. Moses, I think you're being impertinent—and irrelevant."

"You uses words too big for me to understand, but I got your number."

"We simply don't understand one another. I see no point in continuing this conversation. Would you tell your wife I called?"

"Oh, yeah—I gonna tell her. That ain't all I gonna tell her. As far as I'm concerned—and this is plain ol' Willie Moses speakin'—you is finished with J.T."

"Mr. Moses, how can you say that? J.T. is marvelously talented. You can't deny him his gift."

"I can do just what I likes."

Miss Sandor hesitated. "I'm . . . I wouldn't agree entirely."

"What you mean?" His voice was threatening.

"I think a person who has an extraordinary talent can't be treated quite like the rest of us. I mean, he deserves more from those of us who love him and realize his abilities."

All Miss Sandor could hear was low, hard breathing—a convulsive breathlessness of anger rather than of fatigue. She imagined his breath to be hot and sour. She trembled.

"Mr. Moses?"

"I ain't hung up, yet."

"Mr. Moses, you know you can't do anything to alter a God-given gift."

His voice exploded. "I done already told you I can do what I likes."

"But . . ."

"I don't need nobody like you tellin' me, *me*, Willie J. Moses what to do."

"But your son, your son . . ."

"That right, J.T. is *my* son an' don't you forgits it. Mine, mine, mine!"

The phone clicked. Miss Sandor, exhausted, exhilarated and fatigued all at once, sat down on her couch and cried. How preposterous the man was! How unfair of him to want to encroach on the beautiful relationship between herself and J.T. She was still on her couch when the doorbell sounded. J.T. looked puzzled; evidently her face showed that she was upset.

She hugged him so hard he said, "You hug too tight."

"I'm so confused, so confused. Happy and unhappy."

"Like two movements from a composition."

"Yes—only I'm not writing it alone. I'm happy to see you, yet I feel a sense of doom. Do you understand me, J.T.? Julian?"

"Who told you my name?"

"Your father."

He stiffened, and a look of despair spread across his face. "When? Where?"

"Over the telephone. Before you came."

He broke away, and a howl like that of an animal wounded burst from him. He shook his head. Then he began to weep.

"Don't cry, J.T."

She attempted to embrace him, but he backed away from her outstretched hands.

"It can't be that bad, J.T. Really."

"He'll kill us both."

"No, no, I won't let him harm us. Now, don't you worry about a thing, J.T. I'm sure he'll calm down. I feel better myself, now."

"You are reasonable. He ain't."

"Isn't."

"Doubt if it matters now."

"Why do you say that?"

J.T. took her hand and had her sit down on the couch. His face was wet with tears but he had stopped crying. "See, you is real to him now. Before, well . . . well, it was like those fairy tales we read. Now . . ." He sighed. "I just don't know."

"Let's forget it, J.T. Let's play music, listen to music, live music!"

He looked around the rose-carpeted room as if he had lost something. Finally he fixed his gaze on the music satchel he had dropped near the door. Then he smiled.

"Guess what?"

"Tell me."

"Today is my birthday."

"Oh, J.T.!"

"I wrote something for you to remember it by." He fetched his satchel and withdrew some notebook pages. "See." He handed her three pages of a neatly hand-printed composition. "This is for you."

"But, J.T., people should give to you on a birthday. If I'd known . . ."

He hesitated. "There's always next year. C'mon, this is for you to play. See—I got a nice long title after Opus # 1: 'In memory of me for you on my birthday.' "

"That's nice. But, really, you shouldn't say 'in memory of.' That's for after you've gone. We'll change it to 'in commemoration of.' O.K.?"

"Probably don't matter."

"Doesn't. And it does, it matters a great deal."

J.T. placed his composition on the music stand of the piano. He hummed a tune—not his own—tapped one foot on the flowered pattern of the rug, and gazed at Miss Sandor with a detachment that made her shudder.

"I'll play," he said quietly. "I'll play a concert for you today. Listen carefully."

The next day he did not come. She waited and waited but he did not come.

For the first time in months a week passed without Miss Sandor seeing or receiving a word from J.T. or his mother. Miss Sandor began smoking again, a habit she had given up years ago for the only lover in her life. He had abandoned her for marriage to a rich debutante but the memory of their tenderer moments had remained vividly in her mind and still controlled many of her actions. Now, she could hardly remember him.

The tenth day. Each day was counted in terms of when she had last seen J.T. When she could bear it no longer, she telephoned her last two pupils for the day and cancelled their lessons. She bathed, then perfumed herself with some Lilies of the Valley cologne and powder before slipping on her new white dress. She felt it was too early in the season to wear white, yet she liked the straight, simple lines of the pleated skirt folds, gathered at the waist with a rope belt. J.T. would like it, she was sure. She decided against wearing a hat, even though the afternoon sun was blazing fiercely. She wore white gloves. She always wore gloves, no matter where she went.

No one stared at her overtly as she walked down the street towards J.T.'s home, nor did she feel alien amidst the black children, shouting as they played ball, hide-and-seek or hopscotch. The dogs were resting in the shade, the cats in the sun. Two men, leaning against the door jamb of a house-row church ("Jesus Saves" crookedly printed on a painted board tacked above), glanced incuriously at her as she gazed to her left to read the house numbers. She paused before J.T.'s home—a row house like all of the rest, linked together, like sections of an iron chain. A sensation of dread and fear seized her for a moment before she started up the cracked cement steps. A woman, unknown to Miss Sandor but closely resembling Mrs. Moses, opened the door.

"Is Mrs. Moses at home?"

The woman stared at Miss Sandor, then nodded and opened the door wider. "Come on in," she said quietly.

Miss Sandor was led into a large, heavily curtained living room. Although the room was tall and had high windows, it was dark in it and oppressively warm. The venetian blinds were let down to the sill, the slats closed downward, and the worn, silk curtains were partially drawn. This was not a lived-in room, Miss Sandor observed, even though the couch under the front windows, a couch tattered and uncovered, was probably used for sleeping. A cotton curtain—perhaps a large sheet—separated living from dining room. Murmuring voices with a worried tone could be heard by Miss Sandor as she stood like a solitary birch.

"I'll git Lily," the woman said.

Miss Sandor dared to smile. "I'm Miss Sandor."

"I knows who you are. Ain't likely to be no one else, I guess." She pointed towards the couch. "You sit an' I'll git Lily."

The woman disappeared behind the curtain as Miss Sandor sighed and sat upon the frayed center cushion. She held her breath against the fear that once more gripped her. Something was wrong. Then from behind the curtain came a sigh, deadened quickly by the sound of a chair being pushed back. "Oh, Lordy, I reckon I goin' to have to see her," said a voice, Lily Moses'. The curtain was pushed aside by the upsweep of Mrs. Moses' heavy and flabby arms. A broad crucifix in brown, she lowered her arms slowly in a dirginal downbeat.

"You done come," she said.

"I had to."

"You done come too late. O . . ." A wail burst forth as Mrs.

Moses clasped her bosom.

A woman Miss Sandor had not seen before rushed from the dining room and caught hold of the weeping woman. This woman also resembled Lily Moses. Another sister, Miss Sandor assumed. She rose and followed the women into the dimly lit dining room.

"What has happened?" asked Miss Sandor. "Please—you must tell me."

"Oh, it's my Willie who done it, Miss Sandor." Mrs. Moses wiped her eyes and sighed. "He always been mean. But what he done to our J.T. don't compare with nothin' I heard tell of all my life."

"Tell me, tell me what he did!"

The three women stared at her. Then one sister looked down at her hands and spread the fingers wide.

"Done cut off his little finger on the left hand, that's what." The second sister, still holding on to Mrs. Moses, stared at Miss Sandor. "Done hurt the one next to it, too."

Miss Sandor opened her mouth but words would not come. She stepped back, hands to her throat, and bumped into the old spinet piano. How strange she hadn't noticed it when she came in. She put her gloved hand on the scratched surface. The muscles in her head tightened; she felt the blood pounding against her temples. Her voice came out in a whisper.

"You lie, you lie."

She closed her eyes to make the fact of the violence against J.T. disappear. She stifled the impulse to sit and bang out chords and arpeggios on the yellow and dull-black keys. To do so would have soothed her and made her forget.

"Ain't no call to lie 'bout a thing like that, Miss."

Miss Sandor looked up to see who had spoken, but could not tell. Three faces stared at her, like a photograph of three different poses of the same face. She glanced downward and wondered fleetingly at the irony of her choice of a white costume—white dress, white shoes, white gloves—at a time when mourning would have been fitting. She swayed and four hands grasped her and led her to the battered couch. The three of them—Miss Sandor, and Lily Moses' two sisters—sat down as J.T.'s mother moved, dream-like to a large rocker by the wall. A warm breeze rattled the blinds. Suddenly Mrs. Moses began to sing:

> Do, Lawd, do Lawd, Lawd remember me,
> Do, Lawd, do, Lawd, remember me,
> Do, Lawd, do, Lawd, remember me,
> Now do, Lawd, remember me.
>
> When I'm sick and can't git well,
> Lawd, remember me,
> Now do, Lawd, remember me.

Then silence reigned again as the four women avoided one another's gaze. Miss Sandor suppressed the questions raging in her mind. Too late, too late. The answers could not matter now.

She rose and stood before the other women, a stone of white before the black and grieving faces of J.T.'s mother and aunts. Though it was a hot day a chill seized her. She moved slowly towards the piano. Staring down at the yellow chipped keys, she dared to touch and sound out a single chord. It died after a brief, atonal echo.

Miss Sandor turned and retreated from the house without uttering a word of farewell. She rushed down the streets not noticing where she was going. Soon she was at a circle—a statue in its center—and there she sat down on a bench. Automobiles zoomed around her, but she did not notice the din of traffic. Looking skyward, Miss Sandor shivered. She saw the sun but did not feel its warmth. It was as if the sun were transformed into a frosty globe.

She sat and sat, vaguely aware that she would soon rise and return to her quiet, empty apartment. She looked up to find a man staring at her. Slowly his gaze was lowered from her head to her feet. She felt a longing and a revulsion for the questioning interloper. She wanted to leave but dared not move. What did he want? How dare he look at her that way? She would call the police, she would . . .

Miss Sandor rose. There was no use to weep or to cry out her sorrow. Within her there was a sensation of lightness. Of nothingness. Nothingness and sorrow and a terrifying acceptance of the truth. Tomorrow, tomorrow, she said to herself, I will begin again the life I thought to have abandoned. It is still there and awaiting me, O terrible, terrible life.

Born 1933 in Ohio, Margaret Perry currently divides her time teaching and supervising library services at the University of Rochester. She writes short stories, books, articles and book reviews. Ms. Perry has won several prizes for her short stories.

"Didn't mean to offend, but damn it,
when it comes right down to brass tacks,
what in hell are you?

The Ritual Bath

BY LAWRENCE P. SPINGARN

Stirring and ironic . . . a cycle of prejudice.

TONIGHT, Windholz reflected, the priests from the village would bring him the girl—not an ordinary maiden; no, Agoka herself, the chief Ngoru's daughter. It was the highest tribute the natives could offer and, providentially, it coincided with his fortieth birthday.

But as he rested in the wicker chair sipping tea, worry clutched Windholz about the loins. Although he knew her father and appreciated her high standing, he had never actually met the girl. One did not count the time he looked down through foliage to the pool beneath the cascade, where Agoka sat astride a smooth log—his eyes had caressed her brown thighs and full breasts capped by flaring nipples—or the morning she'd passed his bungalow in green silk robes and a white turban, followed by female attendants. It stood to reason that at eighteen, Ngoru's child would be a virgin, though her cleanliness was another matter. And yet, his own houseboys, Tom and Jerry (such were the nicknames bestowed by his predecessor), were prepared: the same huge brass tub he bathed in, with plenty of hot water, soap, and Windholz's scented powder.

Still, he couldn't stand their smell: rank animal sweat. Even at rest, their bodies exuded this jungle stench, and when they'd been running and got near him, Windholz often felt faint. Because of the heat, thank heavens, they seldom ran. The day dripped from his face now and percolated through his reddish-blonde mustache to his crisp khaki shirt, yet it was past four o'clock and winter too. Tea was the thing, however. He'd sooner miss lunch than tea. He'd learned to prefer tea in Cyprus, not so long ago: tea cooled the skin and aided digestion. And tea was superior to whiskey for the nerves. When it came to whiskey, however, he could outdrink the Resident, who was older, very stout, and burned scarlet by the tropics. No, tea was the thing, here in Zambe. One simply stopped work in mid-afternoon to enjoy a cup, to forget where and with whom one lived.

Peering from the verandah, Windholz could see the frontier, not a line but a narrow earthen strip between green jungle walls, and when the air was free of haze, he could make out the bandy-legged Portuguese soldier who manned the control tower. Sometimes he'd heard gunfire at night; the next morning Tom or Jerry would report finding a body nearby, already thick with carnivorous ants. Of course, there was no barbed wire here, as the e'd been before his escape from Italy. He could still remember the words of his indoctrination at Cyprus: the lands ruled by Britain were free, and yet, he thought, puffing industriously at his pipe, control was necessary. One could not permit unschooled blacks to overstep the limits. He treasured the term *Bwana*. For him it was not just a copybook word: in a single grueling year he'd earned the respect of native and white alike. And now when Windholz clapped, Tom appeared instantly—as if he'd been hiding behind the bamboo screen.

"More tea," Windholz ordered. "Plenty hot."

"Yes, *Bwana*."

But when Tom returned with the tray, he wasn't grinning. The jungle telegraph never stopped, and as the boy whispered the news, he too looked displeased. The Resident, Mr. Brooke, was coming. Yes, his jeep had been spotted two villages away. It was rather a game with these natives to spy on the Resident, for whenever he showed up, hoping to surprise the villagers, nothing illegal was to be seen. Today, scant hours before the girl was due, Mr. Brooke had picked an awkward time.

"So," Windholz instructed Tom, "bring whiskey—and ice."

It would take precisely ten minutes, Windholz estimated, for Mr. Brooke to walk through the grove of rubber trees to the house. Of course, he could be driven straight to the verandah: what was he searching for now? Windholz had done his work carefully, honestly. That morning he'd finished his periodic check on the tapping operations. Wanting a mental rest, he'd even balanced his books for the month: however, there were regulations yet undiscovered, and besides, he, Wilhelm Windholz was, technically speaking, an enemy alien—or at best, a stateless person. Perhaps the Resident looked on him with the same suspicion he regarded the natives. Knocking the ash irritably from his pipe, Windholz got up and walked to the verandah steps.

"Brooke?" he called, unable to see far without his glasses.

"That's right, m'boy. How are you, Villy?"

Villy. When would the Resident quit stressing this hard German consonant? It was no longer funny: Windholz had eliminated every trace of accent. And the visitor himself—big, beefy, a barrel of fleshly humors—voiced a false and sickening heartiness. Even in shaking hands, Mr. Brooke held to a subtle distinction: two fingers only, quickly withdrawn. Yes, as if to say: *D.P., once a prisoner in Cyprus, antecedents doubtful. . .*

"The same?" Windholz asked, reaching for the whiskey as Mr. Brooke stretched out on the wicker chaise. It was always the same—in conversation as well, beating about the bush, setting up a barrier of superiority, and, worst of all, laying traps of innuendo: why had Windholz chosen this particular colony, and so close to the frontier at that?

"Thanks, Villy. I caught a thief today. Storekeeper. Robbed the government warehouse and took ammo, mainly. Dangerous these days, ammo—don't you think? Chap was a Parsee, one o' them.

Can't trust Orientals, though many look white, almost as white as we."

Brooke, like most fair men, didn't tan well. His features Windholz noticed, had coarsened with the sun, and his broad nose together with his thick lips gave him a foreign air belied only by his intense blue eyes. A choleric type, he reddened at the slightest effort and spoke with an explosive breathlessness, as if word and deed were to him inseparable. He'd paused and was staring over his glass. He anticipated some comment: Windholz forced out the words.

"Will he be sent to jail?"

"No," the Resident held back, enjoying the pause. "No, he'll be shot for treason. It's still wartime—or haven't you heard?"

Windholz resented the question, the veiled implication of difference. In Cyprus he'd tried to enlist while the Nazis were overrunning Crete. It was impossible, he lacked papers. Now that he had papers, he was tied down to this job managing the plantation. Rubber was essential material, though the war, everyone supposed, was nearly finished.

"That's very severe, Brooke."

"I agree—but in your country, Villy, the fellow would've been tortured first."

"It's . . . it's not my country," Windholz said painfully.

He'd wanted to shout his answer. This wasn't fair, wasn't sporting: the Resident knew full well that he'd left Germany in 1930, before the Terror. He could have answered in Italian; barring Mussolini, he might have adopted Italian citizenship. He spoke Greek also, whereas Brooke hardly spoke his own tongue correctly, especially when he was drunk.

"Sorry, old boy. Didn't mean to offend, but damn it, when it comes right down to brass tacks, what in hell *are* you? Regulations have gummed up everything. We can't really call you a Hun. You're a good chap, Villy, so please tell me—where d'you stand?"

A pipe was convenient, Windholz decided; a fine British pipe. By sucking at the stem, he could look wiser than he felt. 1930: fifteen years had passed, and before that, neighbors in Marienberg, seeing the elder Windholz walk in the Haupstrasse, tall, slender, and distinguished, had agreed that he too was a "good chap," even though born in Poland.

"An enemy alien—that will do, I hope."

"If you insist, Villy, but it sounds rather harsh."

"Then," Windholz said quickly, "let's forget it. Can you stay to supper?"

He wasn't being sincere: the pipe smoke widened the gap between them. Brooke's eyes shifted to the table with its siphon and bottle.

"Can't tonight. Tonight duty beckons. No, I must hurry on and leave you to your pleasures. Cheers!"

When the Englishman left, the buzzing phrase stuck in Windholz's ear. *Pleasures!* Brooke must have known that Agoka was being brought here tonight. Yes, word had gone from village to village in the district. The houseboys had surely gossiped, or the chief himself, for the honor cut both ways: a white man, a *bwana* would deflower Agoka. But when Tom came for the tray, Windholz did not question him. He washed and shaved, changing from work clothes to Hongkong silk pyjamas. Rain began lashing across the verandah. He watched Tom lower the jalousies, then moved to the dining room where the table was set for one and the candles in the seven-branched holder gave forth a faint perfume.

Set for one: he dared not invite the girl. As he gazed at the wine glass, Windholz recalled his grandmother blessing the bread: the same candlestick, the same fluted goblet, only a sweeter wine. The old woman had muttered a pious incantation akin to that of the witch-doctor in the village below: at her death, her son and grandchildren lost the sharp edge of belief. As Windholz bent his head, a disinherited moth brushed against his blonde hair: Marienberg, Anticoli, Nicosia, Zambe. Supper was not quite ready. When he passed to the inner room and saw the bed waiting expectantly on its platform, the covers turned back and the mosquito netting just repaired, his pale eyes were still bemused.

He'd gone long without women, here. Sometimes, however, he'd cross the fr ntier (unlawfully) to Nova Coimbra, a dirty Portuguese settlement where the cafes were crowded with opulent half-castes. It did no good to ask them first: their certificates of health were nearly worthless, like their smiles, like the inflated money they demanded. He could only get very drunk and take his chances with the youngest who offered. The soap and water of purification was his obsession: he saw with dismay that the brass tub was grimy, but there was time after supper, and his glance met another face in the wall mirror: his own, transfigured by the fretful look.

A black girl, that was going far—though in Nova Coimbra the pelts of the half-castes were like velvet, and their liquid eyes, simmering with feigned enjoyment, had fascinated him. His were blue eyes, cornflower blue; a straight, refined nose; a narrow face dignified by the crisp military mustache that men of Mr. Brooke's stamp admired. And once, worming through the battle lines below Rome, he'd been saved by these very features: the S.S. officer, scrutinizing him more closely than his pass, had let him go with a warning. Quitting the mirror, Windholz found the row of trophies on the wall. His blue ribbon from the Officer's Club, another joke, for in winning the tennis tournament, he'd undergone a sort of Anglification: *William Windholt, N.O.C., First, 1943.* When the supper gong sounded, he was smiling.

The house boys were deceived, too, as the British on Cyprus had been. Both served him with more ceremony than efficiency. In the silence of his evening meal, Windholz heard only the faint whisper of rain and the dry scuttle of roaches in the mats of the roof. He had trained Jerry to pour wine correctly: Jerry never profaned the goblet with his touch, he stood as far distant as possible. But neither Tom nor Jerry could yet carve, even from a cold joint of mutton. Now the coffee bubbled in its flask set above the candle. As Windholz finished his second cup, the rain trailed off in a final tired lisp. He was enthroned in the living-room when Tom lugged past him the canister of hot water for Agoka's bath. Five minutes later, a shrill cry from the verandah announced the priests.

The girl, leaning on their arms with closed eyes, was robed from head to foot in soft white cotton. She seemed to have swooned. She would not look up as greetings and presents were exchanged.

To one priest Windholz gave his cricket bat, to the other a frayed necktie in regimental stripe, but the men, grinning happily, were overwhelmed by these trifles. They sat cross-legged in the doorway, waiting for the polite moment to depart, but when they'd gone and Tom had escorted Agoka inside, Windholz felt a sudden depletion. He sought the long chaise on the verandah. He listened to the splashing that came from the tub and next, the swish of the heavy towel. Was Tom dusting her with powder? Would he also remember to spray her with cologne? When he was sure that she was lying on his bed, Windholz gripped the armrests harder. Panic moistened his face and dripped from his chin.

"*Bwana*," Tom called softly, but Windholz did not answer.

Naked, velvety, pearled by sweat—his bride Sophie, twenty years ago, had submitted to the same ritual. Sophie Levin, her wet black hair clinging to her shoulders, blushing as she stepped from the bath; and the rabbi—what was *his* name?—signing the document testifying to her purity within the faith. But Sophie, he'd heard, was dead: gassed in the ovens after another ritual bath. The letter from his uncle in Switzerland, who worked for the Agency, foretold her death. Uncle Max, once an accountant, a wizard at figures; and soon the full story of these horrors would be published, yet Windholz had not deserted Sophie. Never, though he might have divorced her as a barren wife. He might have kept the dowry, too. Instead, a separation, and he'd gone to Italy—in 1930, before the world blew apart.

A white gown: Sophie in white beneath the *huppa*, the awning in her mother's garden, the garden later uprooted by vandals; the house pillaged; rape and ruin everywhere. And this newer bride: he'd seen the broad nostrils, the scarifications on the cheeks, the silver earrings—all much admired in Zambe, yet even with eyes shut, Windholz would smell through talcum and cologne the odor he feared: of moldy vegetation under the rubber trees, of squashed bugs and the ooze from bodies pressed into the mulch of love. If Agoka must wear white, why, then, it would only be momently, until he peeled off the clinging cotton, fondled her breasts, completed the oblation.

"*Bwana!*" Tom called again, standing at the doorway, blinking with amazement at the delay.

"Go to your house, Tom. Leave me alone, all night."

All night? The whiskey he loathed speeded the hours. He could not see as far as the clock ticking on the wall, but could feel the alcohol jumping in his veins, to the heart whose existence Sophie once denied. Wrong, Sophie had been wrong: had he not wept at hearing from Uncle Max? The tears came again; during the interval, Windholz had accepted less and less: Italy, Cyprus, Mr. Brooke's face, the half-castes across the frontier . . . He was becoming drowsy. He was falling, falling through the floor where boards had rotted away. And soon he grovelled, helpless, on the bare strip between the jungle walls. From the watch tower the bandy-legged Portuguese took aim. The shot exploded. His blood was already flowing to the earth.

"Tom! Jerry!"

His own loud terror woke Windholz. Wild-eyed, distraught, his hair crinkly with sweat, he staggered from room to room, pursued by the red vengeance of yesterday's heat. Only when he found the girl asleep on his bed did he realize it was dawn. He lowered his arms and breathed more easily. Yes, Agoka awaited him. Her naked breasts rose and fell rhythmically. Her full lips pouted in a vague smile of peace and forgiveness. He had merely to touch her, to rouse her to his need.

"Sophie," he whispered, thinking back over the long interval to another girl, another country.

Forgetting, though, was his specialty. Within the hour, he guessed, the priests and Agoka's father would return, demanding the bloody sheet as token of her virginity and his manhood. Again, Windholz glanced at the mirror: blonde, above suspicion, ever free to move through enemy lines . . . But who was the enemy now? He felt confused. As he noticed the blue ribbon pinned to the wall, he grimaced at his misspelled name. William Windholt, alien, exile, washed clean of harsh memory, finally accepted. Still, he was falling; falling into the velvet darkness he'd always feared. Blinded by sweat he touched Agoka. When she stirred and opened her eyes, he dropped to the bed.

Lawrence P. Spingarn is a professional short story writer, poet and painter. His stories and poems are published in England and the USA.

"You're looking at yourself with the eyes
of a stranger's envy."

Moments

BY YURI BONDAREV

A series of poignant vignettes.

Unequal Shares

"YOU'LL be good to me, won't you? You won't do anything to
hurt me? Because, you see, I'm so sorry for her!"

"For *her*? Who do you mean?"

"For myself."

"But I love you, you're the only woman in the world for me."

"You'll love me forever? If something happens to me, you will
remember me, won't you?"

"Nothing will happen to you."

"But *if*?"

"All my life. Still, nothing will happen to you."

"You see, in love, too, there's no justice. It gives out unequal
shares. There is no such thing as equal shares in love."

"I don't understand you "

"I was given the bigger share, and you, the smaller. You love me less than I love you."

"What strange arithmetic!"

"No really, the most terrible thing is to get tired of each other. And don't you dare laugh—I think about it so often. If you ever get tired of me, you must leave me at once, without saying a word."

In Front of a Mirror

DURING the New Year party she stopped in the foyer in front of a mirror and there, in the reflected brilliance of the chandeliers, among the well-dressed women, she saw herself so ordinary, so plain and unattractive, that she glanced back at him in fright, turned pale and said quickly:

"Let's go home, please, now!"

He guessed what she was thinking, kissed her on the forehead and said softly:

"You're looking at yourself with the eyes of a stranger's envy."

She dropped her arms in relief and smiled at him with humble gratitude.

"Thank you: I see that you love me after all."

Dialogue on a Seat in the Park

"HAVE you been married?"

"Yes."

"How long ago was it? Well, I mean . . . you are still so young."

"Why, I have a five-year-old son. My husband and I parted."

"Does that mean you didn't love him?"

"If only I didn't love him! But the bitter truth is better than a sweet lie. I would've forgiven him, if only he'd told me the truth. But he lied to me. He tried to justify himself, he explained that it all had taken place in hospital, that she was a doctor and was as different from me as the earth from the sky, that he loved only me. But I couldn't forgive him. I made him turn his back to me and answer my questions. I questioned him and he answered. The most terrible thing of all was that though he cried, he still continued to tell lies. Then he wanted to take our son away . . . He is still unmarried. He comes here every year to have a look at his son . . ."

"It isn't only to have a look at his son, believe me!"

"It's no use. My love is absolutely burnt out: Only the ashes are left."

A Glance

I witnessed this episode at a dance floor just out of town.

Lively and slender, with an aquiline nose and dark eyes that had a violet shade to them, he asked her for a dance with such a fierce and hungry expression on his face, that she was even a little frightened and looked up at him with the pitiful and embarrassed expression of a plain girl who had never expected such an honor.

"Oh, no, no!"

"Per-r-mit me!" he insisted showing his large white teeth in an artificial smile. "I'd be gr-g-eatly honored!"

She looked around as if asking for help, then quickly wiped her fingers with a handkerchief, and mumbled:

"Nothing'll come of it, probably. I'm a poor dancer . . ."

"Never mind! Come on. We'll manage somehow."

He danced impassively, with the air of dandy. He was coldly arrogant and didn't even look at her, while she clumsily shuffled her feet, swinging her skirt and fixing her stare at his necktie. Suddenly she jerked up her head—the couples around them had stopped dancing and had left the dance floor; there were whistles, they were being scrutinized, it seemed, by his friends, who made sarcastic remarks and mimicked her movements, shaking and choking with laughter.

Her partner, with a stone-like face, continued to play the gallant cavalier, but she had become aware of all the unforgivable meanness of this handsome creature. However she didn't push him away from her, nor did she leave the dance floor; she just removed her hand from his shoulder, and, blushing deeply, knocked on his chest with a bent finger as if it were a door. Taken aback, he bent over her and raised his eyebrows questioningly. Without saying a word, she gave him a slow, level look with the imperious and scornful air of an experienced and beautiful woman who is confident that she is irresistible. It seemed to me that his face changed completely, then he let her go and, embarrassed, he somewhat defiantly escorted her to the column where her girlfriends were standing.

She had thick lips and large gray shadowy eyes, that looked a little wild. Yes, she would have been very plain, had it not been for her long dark eyelashes, almost yellow corn-colored hair and that upward glance which turned her into a beautiful woman and which I had never forgotten.

The Steppe

SOMETIMES I try to remember my very first contacts with the world, in the hope that this might take me back to the innocent period of happy surprises, unaccountable exaltation and first love, and give me back those feelings, which later, as a grown up man, I have never been able to experience so clearly and keenly.

To what age do my first recollections belong? And where was it: in the Urals? Or in the Orenburg steppe? When I asked my parents these questions they were unable to accurately reconstruct the details of my early childhood from memory.

Be that as it may, many years later I understood that the instant of the highest happiness caught and, so to say, fixed in one's consciousness is the miracle-making contact of a past moment with the present, of things lost forever with the existing beauty of the eternal, of childhood with adulthood—just as golden dreams are connected with reality. However, it may very well be that my first impressions were only a vague throb of the blood of my ancestors in me, of my great-grandparents, the voice of the blood, which took me back hundreds of years to the time of some kind of transmigration, when at nights the wild wind, a pirate, was raving in the steppes, lashing the grass about in the dove-colored moonlight, and when the creak of many carts on a dusty road mingled with the primordial noise of the grasshoppers which filled with their chirring huge areas scorched by a wicked sun in the day-time so that the air, heavy with the smell of horses, became hot and dry.

But the first thing I do remember is the moist freshness of an early morning, luxuriant grass heavy with dew on the high bank of a river where we camped after travelling what seemed like all night . . .

I am sitting on the grass wrapped in something redolent, warm and soft (probably a sheepskin coat), together with a close group of my brothers and sisters (though I had none), and sitting beside us is an old woman, so quiet, gentle, and homely, also wrapped in something dark (the only thing about her that I remember very clearly is a peasant kerchief on her head). She is bending a little towards us, as if to warm us and protect us from the morning cold with her body. (I see and feel it all very distinctly.) Bewitched, we are all staring at the monstrously huge crimson ball of the sun rising from the grass on the opposite bank of the river; it is unbelievably fiery, blinding us with its dazzling rays, and all of it is reflected in the pink quiet of the water. Happily silent and with a hidden ritualistic joy of expectation, we all fuse with the morning warmth which it is exuding and which we already begin to feel on this dew-drenched bank of a nameless steppe river.

And strange as it may be, I see it all, as if in a film or a dream— the high hill, the grass, the river, with the sun above it, and all of us on that hill, the whole dark group of us bent slightly to the right and wrapped in sheepskin coats to protect us from the morning chill; and our grandmother, or great-grandmother, rising above our group—I see it all as if from aside, but I don't remember a single face. The only thing I do remember is a white, round and kindly blob (rather than a face) under a peasant kerchief; it gives me a childish feeling of security and a vague, tender feeling of love towards her and the beauty of that morning which opened up before me on the bank of the river and which is inextricably bound up with the kind face of my grandmother or great-grandmother, whom I never met later in life . . .

When I remember this little piece of half-dream and half-reality, I am always carried away by a feeling of incredibly quiet happiness, which takes me into its soft embrace as if the tender kindness of the earth, opened up there, at the moment the sun rose from the grass—the sun we saw somewhere on the way, during our long journey to somewhere. To where?

What is even more strange is the fact that I remember the light, the scents, the journey itself, and the feeling of expectation of a slow approach to some unknown and unprecedented beauty, to a Promised Land, where everything was bound to bring happiness.

Also hiding somewhere in the corners of my memory are a gray, rainy day and a large wooden house not far from a crossing over a wide river. And on the opposite bank of the river, on a hill, can be seen the dim outline of a town with churches and orchards. It's not distinct, but it is quite clearly a big town.

I don't see myself—whether I'm in the house or near it. All I remember is a small mound of earth, wet from the rain, along the outer wall of the house, carved window-surrounds, and a road trampled by horses, leading from the house to the river. I feel the murmur of the rain and know that somebody will call me in a minute. All around me, the humid air is filled with the warm smell of horses, horse manure, harness, and the scent of fresh bread— all those wonderful smells, eternal as life and movement, are painfully disturbing to me even now.

But why is all this living in me, a town dweller? The same voice of the blood of my ancestors? After I was a grown man I once asked my mother, when it was, that day, the rain, the river-crossing, and the town on the other bank of the river. She said that it was all before I was born. But I think it would be more correct to say that she just didn't remember that day, just as my father didn't remember a night which has remained in my memory forever.

It was dark and I was lying in a cart on fragrant hay, so heady and honey-sweet that it made my head spin and the black starry sky above my head was spinning too. The sky was both frightfully far away and so huge that it seemed quite near, as it can be only in the night steppe; the sky was pricked with stars that twinkled, moved about, shone bright; constellations were reorganizing according to some secret law, the Milky Way was floating high in the sky like a trail of white, shining smoke.

Down on the earth our cart was swaying along the steppe road and I felt as if I were floating between the sky and the earth, my heart sinking in ecstasy. The other reason for my delight which I couldn't express in words, was that all this dark and starry space of the Universe spread over my head, and the entire darkness of the summer steppe, were packed with the metallic ringing of crickets, so violent, so passionate that it seemed to me that the silvery drilling sound in my ears was caused by the regal brilliance of the scattered Milky Way . . .

The only earthly things around me were the lazily swinging cart, its squeaks and measured movement, the dust stirred up by the wheels, the soft, moist snorting of the horses which were invisible to me from where I lay, the scent of the hay and the agreeable smell of horse sweat. These habitual sounds and smells pushed me back to earth, but at the same time I couldn't tear myself away from the sky which drew me in with its mysterious secrets.

I love everybody, I thought. And everybody loves me. That's how it'll be for the whole of life.

Then my father stirred beside me; I heard him grunt sleepily, and became aware of the smell of his tobacco and clothes, so familiar and strong. Father sat up on the hay, his figure a dim dark silhouette, looked around at the barely visible white road, carefully took a rifle, jerked the bolt open with a light metallic click, took out the clip, wiped the cartridges on his sleeve and pushed the clip back. Then he told my mother in a low voice that there was a village ahead which was not safe: three days ago a man had been killed there. My heart sank and I closed my eyes. It was only several years later that I was able to express in words the feeling of disturbed harmony I had experienced then. I asked my father whether he had killed anybody himself. If so, how did it happen? Was it a frightening thing to kill a man? And why? What did you kill a person for?

When I came back from the war at twenty-one, I didn't ask my father such questions.

But never again did I feel such a oneness with the sky, such silent ecstasy in the presence of the Universe as I experienced then, in my childhood.

The famous Soviet short story writer, novelist and script-writer Yuri Vasilievich Bondarev was born in 1924 in Orsk, a town in the Southern Urals. When World War II broke out, he was a schoolboy who then joined the army. His experiences at the front—the hardships and heroism—remain a major force in his work. He is a graduate of the Gorki Literary Institute and the recipient of the Lenin prize for the motion picture Liberation *(1972), the State prize of the USSR for the motion picture* Hot Snow *(1975), and the State prize of the USSR for his novel* The River Bank *(1977).* The River Bank *is being published in ten countries outside the USSR. "Moments" was translated by Tamara Mats.*